The Margarita Solution

In This Series

The Margarita Solution

Chiseler with a Glass Jaw

When the Contralto Sings

Stalking the Scratch Man

The Tenacious Goldbrick

Cryptic Paisley

The Margarita Solution

The Margarita Solution

Chester Henry

DAGMAR MIURA

LOS ANGELES

Published by Dagmar Miura
Los Angeles
www.dagmarmiura.com

The Margarita Solution

First published 2018

ISBN: 978-1-942267-86-7

ONE

Truman could think of only one solution: margaritas. Drinking would address the immediate issue of his frustration with not getting any gigs lately, but of course it wasn't going to help with the larger issue, the gnawing doubt that he wasn't good enough at it, that his clients didn't like him, and that's why he wasn't working. He pulled out his phone and dialed Celeste, his best friend.

"I have to work tomorrow," she protested. "We can go out on Saturday."

"Saturday is for amateurs. Meet me at that Mexican place on Sunset. I love the bar."

"You love it because there are always cops in there."

"I do not have a thing for cops," Truman said.

"I like it because there's lots of WeHo guys, but it's not a WeHo scene, where I'm not hot enough."

"It sounds like it's still about your libido." She sighed. "See you at nine?"

"Too early."

"I can't be out late. I'll be there at nine."

"Wear something slutty," Truman said, and ended the call.

Stretching out on his bed, he ran a hand through his thick dark hair. He didn't need to style it, he decided. It was only margaritas, and the point wasn't to meet guys. Above him the wooden beams of the ceiling arched toward the wall with the high windows in it, the ancient glass panes distorted and cloudy with decades of dust and air pollution, but there were enough of them to let a lot of light into his loft. A hundred years ago it had been built as a warehouse, or maybe a factory, but today the pillars and the stairs and the lack of space for a truck to pull up made it useless for forklifts and pallets and shipping containers. Industry had moved to roomier digs outside Los Angeles, leaving this place for Truman and a couple of other tenants to spread out.

And there was a lot of room—besides his bed and his desk and a kitchen table for the microwave, he had space for three comfy thrift-store sofas, arranged in a square at one end to make a virtual living room. The downside was the hard lease, which meant he had to put up his own blinds, which he'd never bothered to do, and had to hire his own plumber. Celeste's dad, Ernesto, had rewired the space so that he could plug in his electronics and his coffeemaker. When he'd moved in, there had only been a series of alarmingly oversize industrial sockets. Ernesto had also helped him put up wood framing and drywall around one corner of the room, where the toilet and the shower were, which had made the space a lot more livable. At heart it still looked like a factory—the new walls topped out at eight feet, leaving another six feet of air under the wooden beams of the ceiling.

A dark shirt with a collar, he decided, digging through his clothes rack. He didn't have a body that would ever turn heads, but for a night out, the right pair of jeans maximized what he had to work with. After a last look in the bathroom mirror, he pushed his hair back and pulled on a jacket for the chill of the winter evening, then locked the heavy steel door and trotted down the stairs to the street.

In the daytime the Fashion District buzzed with activity, wholesale and retail and manufacturing, but in the evening the streets were quiet, the shutters rolled down on all the storefronts. The metro was a few minutes away on foot, and Truman walked with the resolute stride of someone who did it a lot. By the time he got to the brightly lit train platform, the air had lost its chill.

Half an hour later, when he walked into the restaurant on Sunset, he saw that Celeste was already here. The place was crowded, as it always was in the evening, with a throng of people waiting for tables near the door, some of them with drinks in hand. The bar was jammed from end to end. It had been here forever, and was still decorated in 1940s style, dark wood and burgundy-upholstered booths, wrought-iron railings, colorful glazed tile on the walls. Celeste had managed to wrangle a barstool, and Truman greeted her with an air kiss when she spun around, then paused to assess her look. Her black hair was down and tucked behind her ears, and the dress, in a dark-blue print, covered her shoulders but showed her ample cleavage.

"I think we need just a little more oomph," Truman said, frowning in concentration and cupping her breasts with both hands, adjusting them upward. "Much better."

"You're the only guy on the planet that I'd let do that," Celeste said.

"See, there's your problem with meeting guys. You need to loosen up."

Despite looking harried, one of the bartenders stopped and jutted his chin toward them across the bar.

4

"A gin and tonic, and a blended margarita," Celeste told him, then turned back to Truman. "It looks like you're going to have to stand."

"That works for me. The tequila will hit my bloodstream faster." He dug in his pocket for a sawbuck and handed it to her. "I'll be right back."

It was easy enough to walk out of the bar area, but to get to the men's room he had to maneuver through the crowd amassed around the doorway. Tapping elbows and squeezing between people, trying not to jostle their drinks, he was most of the way through when he came face-to-face with a cop, tall and beefy, with a buzz cut and a pleasingly snug uniform, headed in the opposite direction.

"You'll have to step aside, son," he said, talking loud over the noise of the crowd.

"I'm not your son," Truman snapped, scowling at him, but he shifted sideways to let him pass. The idiot was in here for enchiladas like everyone else, and that uniform didn't give him bully rights.

When he got back to Celeste, their drinks were waiting on the bar beside their change, a thin pile of singles. Truman picked up his margarita and clinked it on Celeste's highball glass, then took a satisfying slurp.

"You look a little frazzled," Celeste said.

"It's all about my income. I really have to find something else to do."

"The tour-guiding gigs are drying up?"

"I can barely pay the rent."

"The other night my father had the old movie channel on," she said. "I thought of you. The movie was from 1938, and this guy is standing on Hollywood Boulevard beside a bus, wearing a conductor's cap, hawking a tour. 'See the movie stars' houses,' he says."

"I can't believe that was happening so long ago."

"It was right in front of the Egyptian, so it's basically right where you work."

"Did he look poor?" Truman demanded.

"I guess."

"So it's exactly like today."

"Except it was in black-and-white, and the bus was old and rickety." She grinned and poked at the ice in her gin and tonic with the straw. "So what about leading more of the architecture tours, and the history tours? You like doing those better anyway."

"There's just no money in it. I think I need to find a completely new income stream."

"I might be able to get you a day or two a week at the gallery."

"You'd have to take me out of there in a body bag. I'd die of boredom."

"It's not that quiet," Celeste said, furrowing her brow. But she couldn't deny that the cavernous dark space was dead compared to the vibrant energy of the surrounding Arts District. Some days not a single person came in, and she had to lock up and walk around the block just to remind herself there were other people in the world.

Truman's eyes flicked past her shoulder. "I think it's time to present the irresistible dichotomy."

"Where?" she asked quietly.

"Right behind you."

Celeste twisted on her stool and subtly checked out the guy Truman was eyeing. He was standing behind a woman perched on the barstool next to Celeste's, but he seemed to be on his own. A Corona bottle in hand, he was tall and bald and dark-complected, with serious musculature, like an athlete, his pecs bulging under a dark polo shirt. Worn denim revealed the impressive curves of his legs.

He noticed Celeste's gaze and nodded to her.

"Do you like mayonnaise?" Truman said, leaning toward him.

"I guess so." His eyes narrowed. "Are you selling it?"

"No—I just really like mayonnaise. I get the kind with no eggs."

Celeste nodded in agreement. "A sandwich wouldn't be a sandwich without mayonnaise."

The guy laughed, his tone deep. "This is a Mexican restaurant. I don't think mayo is a big part of Latin cooking."

"My mother might disagree with you," Celeste said, holding his gaze.

He looked from her to Truman. "You're both flirting with me. Are you two a package deal?"

"We're an either-or type deal," Celeste said.

"Both equally capable of rocking your world," Truman added.

He laughed again. "No ambiguity with you two. Does this approach work very often?"

"Sometimes," Truman said, and swirled his tumbler.

It usually didn't work, but Truman wasn't going to tell him that. Their irresistible dichotomy was far from irresistible, even though theoretically any available man would have to choose one or the other, as they were both hot. But he'd hooked up with a guy once using the technique, and so had Celeste, and they'd each scored a couple of make-out sessions.

"Sometimes people think we're vampires," Celeste said.

"I could see that," he said, and grinned.

"Hey—where did my drink go?" Celeste said, turning toward the bar.

"The bartender must have taken it," Truman said. "There's a wet ring where you put it down, see? Gin and tonic is clear, and I saw you jam the lime wedge right to the bottom with your straw, under all the ice. To him it probably looked finished."

"You should be a detective," Celeste said, eyeing him, then turned to their new acquaintance. "Hey, mister—do you need a detective? Truman has the power."

"You do that for a living?" he asked, raising an eyebrow.

The tequila had given Truman a buzz, and he nodded thoughtfully. "Oh, yeah. But I'm pretty new at it." He reached up and patted the top of his head. "My fedora is on back order."

Celeste caught the bartender as he went by. "I wasn't finished with my gin and tonic."

"You want another one?" he asked.

"I want that one."

He shrugged and smiled in mock sympathy, then stepped away.

"He's totally not going to comp you a replacement," Truman said.

"I really want to call him a dick," she said wistfully, "but I know that I can't."

"Indeed, that would be a grave mistake."

Their companion leaned toward Truman and gestured with his bottle. "Why's that?"

"For the same reason you never sucker-punch an airplane pilot mid-flight," Truman said, "or slap the person who's driving the car when you're on the freeway. You never want to piss off a bartender—as soon as you do, the fun is over."

"You two really seem to know your stuff."

"It's the first rule of bars," Celeste said. "Don't mess with the bartender."

"Well, I have to say I admire your competency in this field."

Celeste laughed, flipping her hair back, and the guy stepped closer to Truman.

"I actually do need help finding someone," he said, lowering his voice. "Maybe you could look into it. What are your rates?"

Truman drained the last of his margarita and met his gaze. "Five hundred a day plus transportation," he said evenly.

Celeste raised her eyebrows, looking from one to the other. The guy had believed her—he thought Truman really was a detective.

"I could swing that," he said. "Are you licensed?"

"Not exactly," Truman said.

"Licenses are for chumps," Celeste said, raising her voice. "Truman flies under the radar." She stretched out her palm, weaving it left and right, her eyes narrowing. "It allows him to be agile, and stealthy, and get away with stuff."

The guy laughed.

"It's no joke," she said, holding his gaze. "My

homeboy here is very results-driven."

"Truman, is it?" he said. "I'm Grant."

"Celeste," she said, leaning toward them.

Interesting that she used the Spanish pronunciation, Truman thought. Three syllables, ce-les-*tay*. Sometimes with Anglos she copped out and pronounced it ce-*lest*.

Not about to be sidelined, she extended her drooping fingers and let him delicately shake them. Grant must have thought it equitable to do the same with Truman, reaching for him next. Truman dutifully grasped his hand and squeezed, even though he hated when people did that. Now he had to walk around with a sampler of the guy's microbiome on his skin until he could wash his hands.

"Are you a detective too?" Grant asked her.

"I work in an art gallery," she said, "so I can take care of myself."

"I didn't know the art world was that rough," he said, a smile playing on his lips.

"She has an art history degree," Truman said intently, "and she will cut you."

Celeste laughed. "I wouldn't do that. Mostly it's about negotiating discounts, and shooing homeless people away from the front door. I'm not nearly as rough-and-tumble as Truman."

Grant eyed him. "You don't seem rough either."

"Only in bed," Celeste said. "Or so I've heard."

"Stop that," Truman said flatly. "So who's this person you're looking for?"

"Can we set up a meeting to talk about that? Are you around tomorrow? I know it's Saturday."

"I work when there's work," Truman said, and pulled out his phone. "Give me your number."

Grant recited it, then held up a finger, listening. "That's me. I guess my table's ready."

Williams, party of two, the host had called on the loudspeaker. *Williams.* Truman repeated it to himself so that he'd remember.

"Celeste, it was lovely to meet you," Grant said, with a little bow, and to Truman, "Call me. Maybe we can do some business."

Once he was gone, Celeste said, "Well, that certainly got out of hand."

"We know from experience that not everyone responds to the irresistible dichotomy."

"He figured that part out, but why did he believe you were a detective? I was joking."

"Couldn't I be, though?" Truman said. "I should at least take the meeting. I do need work."

"Do you even know what detective work involves?"

"Isn't it just research? I spend lots of time in the library prepping for my history tours."

"This isn't the same as reading books," she said. "Dude asked if you were licensed. What he means is whether you can legally carry a weapon."

"That makes sense." Truman bit his lip.

"The closest you've ever been to a handgun is when you hit on some poor cop."

"Maybe I wouldn't need a gun. If it gets too difficult, I can bail out. Right now I'm at the point where I can't get by anymore showing busloads of people to actors' front gates. Besides, you were talking me up—I'm too sly to have a license, and all that."

"I was just having fun with it, and I'm feeling the gin. I didn't think he'd actually hire you."

"He hasn't. Not yet, anyway."

"Did you catch Grant's last name when they called his table?"

"'Williams, party of two.' It might be his name, or the person he's meeting. He could also have used a fake name, like when you order coffee and tell them your name is Penelope."

Celeste watched him for a moment. "Maybe you should be a detective."

The bartender leaned across and asked her, "Another round?"

"I have to go," she said, with a thin smile, and scooped up most of her change.

Truman slammed the last icy dregs from his tumbler and set it on the bar, then followed her out to the street, pushing through the crowd around the door.

"I should have checked out who Grant was meeting," he said, once they were on the sidewalk. "Why didn't I think of that? Did you happen to notice?"

"The place was so crowded. I didn't even look," she said, her heels echoing on the concrete as they walked. "But Grant is the potential client—why would you be investigating him?"

"Everyone's a suspect until the curtain drops, sweetie."

She laughed. "You'll have to get the gig first."

"Where did you park?"

"I took the metro so I could drink."

"So no ride home."

Celeste looped her arm through Truman's. "Excellent deduction, detective. But you get a companion as far as Seventh Street."

———◆———

Once he'd peeled off his clothes and climbed into bed, and the tequila had mostly burned off, as he was drifting toward sleep, Truman ran through it in his mind. It might be crazy to attempt to track down a person, maybe even dangerous if it was someone who didn't want to be found. In middle school Truman had been the kind of kid who jumped out of the way instead of trying to catch a pop fly in the outfield, where he was inevitably relegated. He had no inclination for sports or other dangerous pursuits.

The best part of it had been the stylish ball caps. Putting eye-black under his eyes had always seemed cool too. Maybe that's what he was considering now—putting on the mantle of a profession he didn't have the skills to perform, doing ratchet drag. Seriously, what was he thinking? That must have been a strong margarita. Half the time he couldn't even find two socks that matched, never mind tracking down a whole person.

TWO

Celeste woke to a knock on her bedroom door.

"I left you some breakfast," her mother called, and soon she heard the front door close. What a delightful sound—it meant she had the house to herself. Both her parents started work earlier than Celeste, and she luxuriated in this alone time before she had to head out.

Pushing herself to sit up, the floor was cold beneath her feet, and she pulled on a pair of socks, then tied her hair back. In the kitchen she found a plate with a couple of slices of toast, a thick layer of avocado spread on top, still warm and delicious, and a little bowl with some chunks of dark citrus fruit, maybe blood oranges. This was definitely one of the upsides to living with your parents. After she'd eaten, she set up the espresso maker and got it going, then went back to her bedroom.

Even though she'd only had the one drink last night, the whisper of a hangover clouded her mind, so she opened her jewelry box and lifted the tray to find a Vicodin, taking it into the kitchen and crushing it between two spoons, then washing it down with the coffee. She licked the bitter residue off the utensils and drained the demitasse cup. Having a slight headache was the thinnest of excuses, and certainly didn't justify taking narcotics, she knew that. But she did it anyway.

Dropping the cutlery and her breakfast dishes in the dishwasher, she got dressed and locked up the house, climbing into her car for the short drive to the Arts District.

———◆———

The smell of coffee pulled Truman into consciousness. He had his coffeemaker set on a timer to fill the loft with that heady morning aroma, and it always managed to wake him up.

For a while he lay in bed, gazing out the hazy windows at the bright daylight, enjoying the warmth under the covers. These windows had been built to illuminate a workspace, not for the view, so they were high in the wall, the bottom panes well above eye level. But it meant he got a good view of the sky, and a lot of light.

Fully sober now, he thought about meeting with Grant. It seemed a little crazy, posing as a detective. But he had no gigs today, or any lined up for next week, and the specter of financial disaster loomed—he really needed to work. He'd do it, he decided. If Grant's ask was too strange, or it got too hairy, he could bail out.

Climbing out of bed, shivering in the cold air, he poured from the coffeemaker's carafe and climbed back into bed with the steaming mug, sitting up and sipping at it for a while, then setting it on the bedside table and scooping up his phone. Grant answered after a couple of rings.

"I'm glad you called," he said. "You and your girlfriend were certainly having fun last night."

"She's not my girlfriend," Truman said. "Just an old friend. We always chase the same kind of guys."

"Nice that you can do that and still be friends," he said, and chuckled. "So can we meet today?"

"I have some work to do this morning, but my afternoon is open."

"This afternoon, then," Grant said. "Can you swing by my place?"

Truman put him on speaker so he could thumb-type the address into his phone. "Is that an office, or your pad?"

"I mostly work out of my house. It's near

Crescent Heights and Sunset."

"That's where the Garden of Allah was," Truman said. "For thirty years it was the epicenter of film-industry debauchery and intrigue. It was the last place F. Scott Fitzgerald stayed in LA."

"You sound like public television."

"Just some trivia," Truman said, and ended the call. He really needed to shift out of tour-guide mode.

After a swig of coffee, he dialed Celeste.

When she answered, he said, "Where can I get business cards printed up fast?"

"Truman, I'm not your PA. I'm at work."

"How many customers are crowding up your gallery right now?" he demanded.

Celeste looked around the yawning empty space, gloomy except for the spotlights aimed at each of the massively overpriced oil paintings arrayed on the walls. The only sign of life was the murmur of the owner's voice, upstairs in her office on the mezzanine, trying to drum up business.

"A few," she said. "So you're really going to talk to the buff baldy."

"His name is Grant."

"I remember. I'm curious to hear who he wants you to find."

"You could find out in real time. Want to come with?"

Celeste chuckled. "I already have a job.

Besides, I think you're more likely to get some action from him than I am."

"Why do you say that? He wasn't interested in either one of us last night. The irresistible dichotomy rolls snake eyes once again."

"I'm not so sure. He didn't look at my cleavage even once. I think he was way more interested in you."

"I didn't notice that," Truman said.

"Of course you didn't," she said. Truman never felt like the fifth wheel. But she knew she shouldn't be resentful; sometimes it went the other way, and he was the one left out, even if he didn't notice.

"Do a search for quick-copy shops," she said. "They can usually handle stuff like business cards. There's one over here, but I'm sure there'll be one closer to you."

"Thanks, cutie," he said, and climbed out of bed, finally warmed up enough by the coffee.

Celeste was right, he found, once he had some clothes on and had pulled open his laptop. There was a copy-and-print shop just a few blocks from here. Pulling on a jacket and his backpack, he went out, pausing to lock the heavy steel door.

Whoever had subdivided this building must have had a bomb shelter in mind, as the walls and doors were thick and impervious to sound— the only time he heard his neighbors was when someone dropped something heavy on the concrete floor, and the whole building reverberated. Even the windows had wire mesh embedded in the glass panes, a 1920s security measure that still worked—none of them had ever broken.

The gritty streets of the Fashion District were clotted with vehicles, the sidewalks a riot of pedestrians. Walking to the print shop, Truman dodged porters with rolls of fabric, tourists stopped to peer in retail doorways, grubby and disheveled homeless people spare-changing him or digging for bottles in the garbage cans.

The print shop was easy to spot, with foot-tall red lettering in the window that said COPIES, and above that, ENVÍOS A TODO. Truman didn't know exactly what that meant; package shipping, maybe, or money transfers? When he stepped into the shop, the door rattled a little bell that was suspended above it. The only person inside was behind the counter, sitting in front of a computer, a swarthy college-age guy with carefully coiffed black hair. Surrounding him was a jumble of other desks, computers, and oversize printers.

The guy called out something in Spanish when he heard the door, but when he looked up and caught sight of Truman, said, "What can I help you with?"

"I need some business cards printed," Truman said, approaching the counter.

"Do you have a digital file?"

"No, but I know what it needs to say."

"Design costs extra," the guy said, raising his eyebrows.

"There's not much to design. It just needs words on it, no pictures."

The clerk handed him a sheet of paper and a pen, then stepped away.

Truman drew a rough oblong box, and within it wrote his name, and below that, "discreet investigations," with his phone number and his email.

The clerk came back over when Truman set the pen down. He studied the sheet.

"Truman Boudreaux. That's quite a mouthful."

"It's French," Truman said sharply, scowling at him.

"Your work is spying on cheating spouses?"

"I hope not. That doesn't sound very ethical."

"So you're printing these on spec?" he said, frowning.

"I'm kind of new at this job."

"Then why not drop the 'discreet'? To me that makes it sound like a sex thing."

"Fine," Truman said flatly. "As long as it looks simple and stylish."

"My specialty."

"How long will this take?"

"Not long. Go get a coffee."

That was probably good advice, Truman

thought, walking out. No way did he want to be mistaken for the kind of guy who peeped through window shades.

On the next block he found a lunch wagon parked at the curb, a couple of day laborers already waiting for grub. It wasn't upscale enough to be called a food truck, but when Truman stepped up to the window, the guy knew what "vegan" meant, despite the language gap. In a couple of minutes he had three rice-and-bean tacos in hand, which he savored on the sidewalk before walking another block to a coffeehouse. Sitting on a stool at the front window for a few minutes with an espresso, he watched the bustle of the neighborhood.

Eventually he decided it had been long enough, and he walked back to the print shop.

The clerk rose from his desk when Truman stepped in, then presented him with a stack of cards, bound with an elastic band, the top one loose for inspection. It read:

TRUMAN BOUDREAUX
INVESTIGATIONS

"Right on," Truman said, poring over it. "These are so elegant."

"I'm glad," he said, and grinned.

"How much?" Truman asked, and dug out a credit card.

The clerk gave him the total and took his

card, then went to the register. A moment later he stepped back, handing Truman the card. "Unfortunately, the bank says this is declined."

"Ouch," Truman said, feeling his face heating up, and dug out another. "Try this one." As the clerk went to swipe it, he added, "I guess I'd better get some gigs with these business cards, huh."

He didn't reply, but after a moment said, "That one worked."

After he put the stack of cards in his backpack and thanked the guy, Truman walked to the metro and rode to Hollywood, waiting for a bus outside the last stop. The map on his phone showed that Grant's address was near Sunset, as he'd said, but in reality it was closer to Fairfax than to Crescent Heights. Grant probably wasn't confused about the geography; lots of people wanted to be associated with more expensive neighborhoods. If the ads for apartments were to be taken literally, half of LA County was "Beverly Hills–adjacent."

The bus took him as far as Fairfax, and he walked up Grant's street, lined with midcentury bungalows with sprawling front lawns. These people definitely had money. In Celeste's neighborhood, every yard had security fencing around it, and the houses had bars on the windows; in comparison this block looked like the countryside.

Just as he'd zeroed in on which house was Grant's, a huge red antique car slowed and pulled into the adjacent driveway. It had a white convertible top, folded up for the cool weather, and when the engine died, Grant pushed open the long door and stepped out of the behemoth. Today he was dressed up, in a gray satin shirt, black pants, and expensive-looking Italian shoes. In one hand he held a black zippered folio case.

"What kind of car is this?" Truman asked, walking up the driveway.

"It's an Eldorado."

"It's longer than two normal cars stacked together, but it only has two doors."

"In its day it was considered sporty," Grant said. "It wasn't for hauling kids to school and taking their grandparents to the mall—you were doing something fun, like going on a date."

"When was its day?"

"1973."

"It looks great."

Grant raised an eyebrow. "I'm glad you approve."

"It must be expensive, though, to maintain an antique car."

"The word to use is *classic*," Grant said. "It's a classic car."

Truman nodded and looked over the vehicle. "It suits you."

"How's that?"

"Well, it's big, and muscly, and sleek, like you."

"I'll take that as a compliment," he said, grinning and walking toward the door to the house. "What do you drive?"

"I have people drive for me," Truman said, following him.

"You use a car service?"

"I take the metro."

Grant glanced at him quizzically as he reached for the door. He didn't use a key—above the deadbolt was as small keypad, and Grant punched in a code, eliciting the soft click of the bolt retracting. He didn't even try to conceal what he was doing, and from where he was standing, Truman could easily see the numbers—3, 7, 9, 1. It was probably shady of Truman not to avert his eyes, and he knew he should probably instantly forget the code, but before he could, it twigged: those numbers were his car's birthday, in reverse. That seemed like pretty lax security, he thought, following Grant through the doorway, and it was definitely sloppy of him to let Truman see it.

The burglar alarm sounded a strident high-pitched warble, and even though Truman was standing at an oblique angle while he waited for him to disarm it, he could see what Grant was punching in at the control panel—top row, third row, third row, top row—it was the same damn code. Using it twice would make it easier to remember, but still.

Grant set his bag on the kitchen counter and stepped back into the main room, which was carpeted in charcoal gray, with white drapes, decked out with a matching sofa and easy chairs.

"Have you lived here long?" Truman asked, taking it in.

"I just took possession a few weeks ago."

That might explain why it looked a little sterile, Truman thought, but he didn't say that.

Standing there facing him, Grant said, "So what was all that about the Garden of Allah? I've heard of it, but it was torn down before either of us was born."

Truman met his gaze. "I've done some reading about local history. It's an interesting neighborhood."

"It's a great neighborhood," Grant said, resting his hands on his hips, revealing his firm perfect pecs beneath the sheen of his shirt. "At one time the area was middle-class, but now there's nothing on this street for under one-point-five."

"Million?" Truman said dubiously. "For these crummy little bungalows?"

"Real estate is all about location," Grant said, his brow furrowing.

"Are you a real estate agent?"

"Good guess, detective."

"It's not a big leap. Real estate people always say things like that when places are overvalued."

"Well, at your economic stratum, I'm sure it seems out of reach."

"You don't know me, you condescending ass," Truman snapped. "This is still a postwar bungalow, not the Spelling mansion."

Grant's eyebrows shot up. "I didn't mean to offend you," he said, his tone even and amiable. He studied Truman for a moment. "Let's start over. Do you want something to drink?"

"Water's fine," Truman said, stifling his ire.

As he went into the kitchen, Truman took a closer look at the main room. The furniture echoed midcentury design, but it was contemporary, soulless and bereft of character. Grant had definitely hired a designer. Near the front door was a bathroom, with a trendy-looking sink and a loud cactus-print shower curtain filling the back wall.

"One bath?" Truman called to him, peering inside.

"The second one's in the master," Grant said, returning with two water glasses in hand.

"It's strange that this one has a tub in it. It's so crowded, and right at the front of the house. It feels like it should just have a shower."

"Two full baths makes the house worth more."

Truman sighed and followed him toward the living room furniture. "I know your industry has a bathroom fetish."

Grant laughed and set the glasses on the coffee table, then dropped onto the sofa. Truman took the adjacent chair and set his backpack between his feet.

"Who's the person you're looking for?" Truman said.

Grant's expression shifted, becoming serious. "So, last year my sister passed on to her greater reward."

Truman had to think for a second to figure out what that meant. "I'm sorry to hear that."

"Thanks. It was a shock to all of us. She was married to a guy named Martínez, first name *hy-mee*."

Pulling his notepad out of his bag, Truman said, "Can you spell it?"

"He's Mexican, so the *h* sound is spelled with a *j*, Jaime. We also called him Jimmy."

"That's pragmatic," Truman said, glancing up as he scribbled notes.

"Jaime has kind of disappeared."

"Kind of?"

"I heard that he's still in LA, but I can't get hold of him. His phone number isn't working anymore, and he's not staying where he used to."

"Were you close to him?"

"In the way anyone is with their brother-in-law, I suppose."

Truman looked up. "Why do you need to talk

to him?"

"The estate isn't settled," Grant said, gesturing vaguely, then reached for his water glass and took a sip. "He needs to sign some paperwork."

"If it's about paper, shouldn't you get a lawyer to go after him?"

"I need to find him first."

Jotting notes, Truman said, "What was your sister's name?"

"Catherine."

"Did she go by Martínez, or was it still Williams?"

Grant's eyes narrowed. "Her name was Williams."

Truman nodded. "Where did they live?"

"They moved around a bit, but the last address I had for him was in Westlake."

After he wrote down the details, Truman met his gaze. "How did your sister die?"

"Cancer," he said. His tone was earnest. "It happened fast."

"Do you think maybe Jaime wants to be alone so that he can mourn?"

Grant scowled. "He's had long enough to do that. Plus he's not really a one-woman man."

"What does that mean?"

"He plays the field."

"Did he cheat on your sister?"

"It was before they were together."

"So you knew him then?"

Grant waved his hand impatiently. "It was just something she told me once. The point is, I'm sure he will have moved on."

"What does Jaime look like? Do you have a photo?"

"I don't, but he's pretty distinctive: tall, skinny, short hair, dark like Latin folks are, and he used to have a mustache. There's a little white scar over his eye," he said, and touched his forehead.

Writing it all down, Truman nodded. "Where did he use to hang out? Restaurants, bars, maybe a gym?"

"That's a good question." Grant looked thoughtful. "They used to dine on the plaza, at one of the restaurants there."

"What plaza?"

"Sunset Plaza. Right up the road."

That was pretty freaking arrogant, in a city of ten million people, to talk about a thumbnail-size strip of retail as if it would be universally recognized by anyone from outside this neighborhood. But Truman held his tongue.

"What does he do for work?"

Grant sighed. "Not a lot. My sister had the income. He dicked around as a courier and a driver, that kind of thing. Unskilled labor."

"What else can you tell me about him? Interests, hobbies, anything like that?"

"He's slippery," Grant said. "So watch your back."

"Slippery how?"

"I'd say he's one of those people who does what he can get away with, rather than what's right."

"OK," Truman said evenly, and watched him for a moment, not bothering to write that down. "Does that mean he's a criminal or something?"

"It just means that he's slippery." Grant set down his water glass. "So what are your qualifications, Truman? How long have you been doing this?"

"Well, I didn't go to detective school, if that's what you mean." He set his pad on his lap and sat back. "I haven't been in the field for very long, but I'm good at finding things."

It was pure bluster, but there was no way he could tell the truth—everything he'd said and done today was predicated on a lie.

"I guess we'll see," Grant said. "Before you ask, I have some money for you."

Rising, he went into the back of the house, returning a moment later with a sheaf of hundreds, handing them to Truman. Taking the bills, Truman tried not to look startled.

"That's a grand," Grant said, "So two days' work, correct? Let's see where we are after that."

Stuffing the cash in his backpack, Truman

saw the bundle of business cards. He'd forgotten about those. Pulling one out of the stack, he rose and handed it to Grant.

"Boudreaux," Grant said, examining it. "That sounds Cajun."

"I don't think so. That branch of my family came from Massachusetts."

"So how are you going to track this guy down?"

"Let me worry about that," Truman said, holding his gaze. "I don't ask you to lay out your real estate methods." He pulled on his backpack and moved toward the front door.

"Fair enough," Grant said, following him. "I can't believe you don't have a car. Do you need a ride somewhere?"

"Don't worry about that either," Truman said firmly, pulling open the door. "I'll be in touch."

Bluster, plain and simple, he thought, striding to the sidewalk. In reality he had no idea how he was going to approach this.

THREE

A few minutes later, walking into a coffeehouse around the corner on Sunset, Truman was still chafing at Grant's faux concern about his carless state. People who always drove had no idea how to get around without their own wheels, and even though their cleaners and busboys did it every day, they assumed it was next to impossible, like trying to get across the Sierras in flip-flops. In Grant's eyes, not having a car meant he was either stupid or incompetent or impoverished. Part of that was true, Truman had to admit; these days he was way too broke to have his own ride.

Caffeine is what he needed, as well as time to parse everything Grant had told him, time to think it through. He got a double espresso and found a table facing the window. After a few sips of the magic elixir he pulled out his notes and read through them. It seemed like a straightforward ask, but a couple of things didn't quite make sense. Was it odd that Grant didn't have any photos of his sister's husband? And why would Jaime be completely out of touch? Was he consciously avoiding him? Truman probably should have asked about that, whether there was some reason he didn't want to deal with Grant. Why hadn't he thought of that at the time?

Flipping back to the top page, he sighed and muttered, "I'm not a freaking detective."

The woman at the table facing him looked up from her laptop and smiled.

Truman averted his gaze and pulled open his backpack, catching a glimpse of the C-notes as he slid the notepad back in. Even though he had no idea how to track someone down, that cash would be extremely useful right now. Maybe he needed to use it as a motivator.

The only solid lead he had was Jaime's former address. That was where he had to start. He could handle this, he decided, and it wasn't just the rush of caffeine making him overconfident.

Draining his little cup, Truman rose and pulled on his backpack, then headed for the bus stop. Jaime's last digs were in Westlake, and that was right on the way home.

There were more houses in the neighborhood than he had expected. Passing through Westlake, he'd always thought of it as a sea of densely packed apartment buildings, but he knew a century ago it had been a tony neighborhood on the outskirts of the city, home to wealthy oil barons and the big names in the early film industry. *You're not a tour guide today,* he reminded himself. The street he was walking on had some nice Victorians, tightly spaced but not too neglected, and the whole neighborhood was built on rolling hills. Why had he never noticed that before?

Approaching the address Grant had given him for Jaime, he found a run-down house, more dilapidated than its neighbors, with an iron fence around the small front yard. The clapboard siding was probably original to the early twentieth century, but it was in dire need of a paint job. Every window had bars, and it looked like there were two front doors. The narrower one must lead to the upper floor, he realized, meaning the house had been subdivided long ago.

It didn't make sense that people who presumably shared Grant's social status, people who dined out on tony Sunset Plaza, would live in a rat hole like this. Truman double-checked what he'd written on his notepad, but this was the address Grant had given him.

The gate was unlocked, and Truman rattled it before he stepped inside, pausing and listening in case there was a dog guarding the yard. But there wasn't, and he pushed it open and crossed the barren space. The ground had patches of green where the winter rains had brought the erstwhile lawn back to life, but mostly it was hard-packed earth.

Truman rang the bell at the door to the downstairs unit and listened, then rang again. Someone was moving around inside, so he stepped back. Finally a man opened the inner door, leaving the barred metal screen between them. It was dark inside but Truman could see his face, weathered and lined, framed by gray hair. Stepping closer to the screen, he said something in Spanish, a string of words that was something other than a greeting.

"I'm sorry, I don't understand."

"What do you want?" the man asked.

"I'm looking for a guy who used to live here. Jaime Martínez."

"I've never heard of him."

But his reaction betrayed his words—a slight recoil, the spark of recognition in his eyes.

"I know you're lying," Truman said evenly.

The man grinned. "You don't look like the guys he's usually involved with. Did he steal your tricycle?"

"Who is he usually involved with?"

"Not fresh-faced white guys who look like they work behind the pharmacy counter."

"Interesting that you should say that," Truman said, thinking quickly. "I'm with the city health department, and I need to have a word with Mr. Martínez."

He frowned. "I thought the health department was the county."

"Well, when things go sideways, they pull in all the resources."

"You're a nurse?"

"I'm a public health counselor. It's like a nurse."

The guy studied him. "Does he have Ebola or something?"

"I can't divulge the nature of the issue. That's confidential information." Truman stepped closer to the screen and lowered his voice. "I got his name from a former sex partner. I really need to talk to him."

"Seriously? I guess I shouldn't be surprised. He's a real ladies' man. What is it, the clap?"

"I already told you that's privileged, sir. But I can say that it's urgent we put a stop to the transmission of the disease. How well do you know him?"

"I don't know him at all," he said, throwing his hands up. "He rented a room here for a few months, and there were a lot of women in and out."

"When was that?"

"In the spring. He moved out in June."

"Do you have a number for him, or maybe know where he hangs out?"

He sighed. "I know one of his girlfriends from the neighborhood. I'm pretty sure she has an apartment at the Highland Arms. Three blocks down, on the other side of Third. I used to see his car around there sometimes."

"What's her name?" Truman said, pulling out his phone and thumb-typing the details.

"That, I don't know. I never talked to her. I've just seen her around."

"With Jaime?"

"She visited him here. Quite a looker, so I remembered her. Half blond and half brunette, and curvy—a solid rack, you know?" He cupped his hands in front of his chest, stretching them outward for emphasis. "A few weeks later I saw her at the Highland Arms, opening one of the mailboxes. That must mean she lives there."

"Excellent. That might help. You said you know what his car looks like?"

"It's pretty unique. A '72 Road Runner. It's painted matte black."

As he typed, Truman said, "Seventy-two means 1972?"

"Yes," the guy said, and frowned, as if that were a stupid question. "It would look better if he gave it the original paint job. They didn't do matte back then."

"You've been extremely helpful," Truman said.

"Is there a finder's fee?"

Looking up, Truman held his gaze. "You've done a public service in the war on STDs. That should be its own reward."

"So does he have symptoms, or is he just a carrier? Is that how the clap works?"

Truman had no idea, and wasn't even sure what the clap was. Sliding his phone into his pants, he put his hands on his hips, the way Grant had done, projecting authority. "Diseases are a mystery. Sometimes you don't even know which ones you're carrying around."

Turning away, he walked out of the yard, taking a deep breath once he'd closed the gate. It was a great lead, tracking down someone who might know where Jaime was, and he'd even gotten a description of his wheels. But it was getting dark, the long shadows of the end of the day stretching up the houses. He'd follow it up tomorrow. Right now he wanted to get those lovely C-notes into the bank.

The map on his phone told him where the metro was, and he walked that way. Soon he was climbing up out of the ground downtown. The bank machine took the bills, eating all of them blithely, and added them to his account, as if they were real. That had to be a good sign.

———◆———

Back in his loft, Truman sprawled out on the sofa that faced the windows. It wasn't the most comfortable of the trio; that was the purple one against the wall. But this one was good to work on, with an armrest that supported his laptop in the right position. After dark there wasn't much of a view from his windows, just the roof line across the street and the air glow of the lights of the city above it, gradually fading into blackness higher up.

First he paid some bills with his newfound money, then made notes about his meeting in Westlake. He probably should have asked the guy that answered the door if he was the landlord, but that wouldn't have jibed with posing as a bureaucrat; the health department wouldn't ask a question like that. But he admitted Jaime had lived there. If Jaime was sleeping around as much as the guy had implied, he had definitely moved on from Grant's sister.

On the map, the Highland Arms turned out to be a real place, right where the guy had said it was. From the street view it looked like an aging courtyard apartment building, like so many in the neighborhood, two dozen or so units surrounding a concreted common space, all the apartments' front doors outside and facing the yard. The mailboxes were right up front and in the courtyard, which explained how Jaime's old landlord might have seen his girlfriend—anyone walking by on the sidewalk would have a clear view of that space.

The car that the guy said Jaime drove was called a Road Runner. Scrolling through images of the 1972 version, he saw that it was a sporty-looking two-door with a long hood. Interesting that Grant had an old car as well—it must be a family hobby. Classic cars, Grant had called them.

The buzzer at the door sounded, and Truman checked the time. It was after six. He knew who it was. Grinning to himself, he got up and pressed the button to unlock the entry door downstairs, then flipped open his deadbolt. Moments later Celeste breezed in, still dressed for work.

"Do you want a beer or something?" Truman asked.

"Have you got any of those fancy Italian sodas?" she said, and flopped on the purple sofa. As Truman went to the fridge to grab one, she called after him, "I can't figure out why you buy those when you're broke."

"If you're so worried about my finances, save me a dollar and don't drink it," he said, handing her the bottle.

She chuckled and twisted off the cap. "So how was your date with Grant?"

Truman dropped onto the adjacent sofa. "He lives right by Fairfax, but he has a bougie attitude about it, like it was freaking Bel Air."

"We know Truman hates bougie."

"I don't hate it, but it bugs me when people feel they have to condescend to me to demonstrate their superiority. The guy lives in a damn bungalow. It would probably fit inside this loft. West Hollywood was settled as an aspirational suburb in the postwar housing boom. It's not some exclusive enclave. There used to be freight trains running down the middle of Santa Monica Boulevard."

"Tru," she demanded. "Focus. This is not a tour-guide job."

"Right." He grinned. "Detective work doesn't require the historical context. He wants me to find his brother-in-law."

After Truman had told her Grant's story, she said, "Are you actually going to try to find the guy?"

"He gave me a thousand bucks up front, and a good chunk of it is already spent. I kind of have to work for him now."

"Right on," she said, and raised her bottle, tilting the neck toward him. "Even if you can't produce results, you've already been paid."

"In cash, no less."

"That seems appropriate. Is it in small bills? You should throw it up in the air and let it fly all around your loft."

"It's already in the bank. Ten C-notes wouldn't make much of a cash storm anyway."

She nodded. "Plus you probably can't afford to lose any of them under the bed or on top of the ducts."

They talked a while longer, and Celeste finished her soda.

"You're so energized right now," Truman said, rising from the sofa, "but I've got to get an early start."

"So you're throwing me out."

"Or maybe I'm giving us both the gift of being well rested."

Celeste rose and gave him a brief hug on her way to the door.

"Are you working tomorrow?" he asked.

"Unfortunately. Call me if you find out anything fun."

After he prepped his coffeemaker and set the timer, Truman peeled off his clothes and climbed into bed. It got pretty dark in here, except for the constellation of indicator lights on all his electronics, the TV and the router and the tuner, and the ambient urban light through the high windows. Even in the dark there was so much going on out there, people running around and doing stuff, regardless of whether he was asleep or not. When he focused on it, he could hear it happening, the constant low rumble of the metropolis.

———·———

Awake before the coffee started, Truman rolled out of bed and switched off the timer. There was stuff to do, no time to dawdle and wake up slowly, not today. After he got dressed and ate a bowl of muesli and an apple, he pulled on his backpack and headed out.

The central library was half an hour's brisk walk, and Truman admired the building as he came up on it, a glamorous 1920s temple to wisdom, capped by a brightly decorated pyramid. In the lobby he stopped at the café to slam an espresso, then headed downstairs into the bowels of the modern wing.

Before he went to the research desk, he stopped at a terminal to do a search of the library's catalog to find books on detective work. Once he was standing in the relevant stacks, he cocked his head to read the spines, pulling a few volumes out to flip through and scan the contents, finally settling on one that felt right: Biff Sturgis's *Eleven Steps to Becoming a Hard-Nosed Detective*. The worn clothbound hardback had that scent of old books, and Truman checked the publication date.

It had been on these shelves since the 1930s, but surely the essential elements of the work couldn't have changed that much. Tucking it into his bag for later, he headed downstairs to the research desk.

A brief conversation with a librarian gave him some avenues to search for Jaime in various databases. Truman wanted to look into Grant as well. Finding a quiet desk away from the counter and near the stacks, he sat down and pulled out his laptop.

Both men had such common names that it soon became apparent he wouldn't easily be able to pin them down. Lots of people with those names came up in court cases, but there were no photos to clarify who they were. When he researched Grant's address, a real estate site said that the most recent sale of the house was to someone with a completely different name: M. R. Wilson. Was Grant just renting the place? But he'd talked about it as if he were the owner, and he was in the real estate business. It didn't make sense.

Truman sat back in his chair and thought it through. Maybe Grant had bought the place in someone else's name for some financial reason. People with money always found loopholes and tax dodges like that. It was also possible, he realized, that Grant had lied about his real name.

Social media provided nothing informative either, as there were dozens of people with Grant's name, and with the even more common Wilson name. Searching for Jaime's name felt like an even more insurmountable task because most of the hits were in Spanish.

Rubbing his eyes, he tried the last database the librarian had turned him on to: a list of people who got property-tax exemptions. Grant was nowhere to be found, but Jaime's name came up, along with an address. Checking on a map, he sat up in his chair when he saw where it was—right in Westlake, a few blocks from where Jaime had lived, on a busy boulevard. The street view showed a small liquor store in a one-story building. Grant hadn't said anything about that, but the proximity implied it might be the right person.

Poring over the database entry again, he realized there were two addresses—the liquor store with the tax exemption and a separate mailing address. That one was in Boyle Heights, or near it, where Celeste lived. The street view showed a block-long building with a sign out front proclaiming it to be a seniors residence.

Sitting back, Truman stared at the screen. Jaime was no senior, but maybe it wasn't just a senior's lodge, or maybe he worked there. But the database said it was his "address of residence." If he wasn't really working, as Grant had implied, was it logical that he owned a liquor store? Maybe he just owned the building, and the store's rent meant he didn't have to work. If he had that kind of resources, though, why had he been renting a room in a flophouse?

Truman sighed and rubbed his eyes. He had to go to the Highland Arms in Westlake today, and he could check out the liquor store at the same time, but maybe he could swing by the seniors residence first. It took a minute to assess what bus he should take from the metro station at Mariachi Plaza, but once he'd figured it out, he packed up his computer and then signed out his *Hard-Nosed Detective* guide, stuffing it into his backpack and heading up to the street.

On the train he got a seat and pulled out his library book. A few of the chapters covered things he hoped he wouldn't have to do, like "How to Throw a Punch" and "Compiling a Sucker List." Some sections he had to read through to figure out what the author, Biff Sturgis, was even talking about. "How to Pack a Heater," it turned out, covered how to carry a handgun, and "The Art of the Kovac" explained how to slap someone around effectively while fending off retaliation. Truman sighed and flipped to "Biff's Basic Principles."

Once he'd climbed up out of the ground and transferred to the bus, he left the book in his bag and watched the city roll by. The seniors residence was at the fringe of Boyle Heights, he realized, if this was still Boyle Heights. The vibe of the neighborhood was a mix of industrial and residential, which made him wonder what it been like a hundred years ago. This close to downtown, it had definitely been used for something.

The bus dropped him a block from the seniors residence, and walking up on it, he found it was a midcentury low-rise. The fine print on the sign out front read CLASSY ASSISTED LIVING. That struck him as a red flag. *Classy* was one of those words, like *upscale* and *exclusive* and *prestigious*—if you had to proclaim it yourself, it probably wasn't true. At close range the coat of fresh white paint certainly wasn't concealing the sagging roofline, and the bars on the windows didn't really evoke elevated social status. Faux marble flanked the main entrance, and that neoclassical pediment above it wasn't fooling anyone.

Inside, the place looked like a hospital, and it seemed quiet, apart from a blaring television somewhere down the hall. A woman in scrubs with her hair bundled atop her head sat behind the front desk.

When she looked up from her screen, Truman told her, "I'm looking for Jaime Martínez."

She frowned. "You mean Jamie?"

How Anglo was that, Truman thought,

mangling it that way. He grinned and said, "Some people call him Jimmy too."

"Are you a relative?"

"By marriage, yes."

"He's in 122." She gestured down the hall. "Right and right again."

"So he's here," Truman said, surprised.

Her eyes narrowed. "Why wouldn't he be?"

"Thanks," he said, stepping away before he got drawn into an interrogation.

Maybe that's why Grant had lost track of him—Jaime was in nursing care. Maybe he was one of those Medicare hostages, just sick enough for the facility to keep him sedated for months and months, to keep the payments rolling in, but not lucid enough to contact his family or call his brother-in-law. Truman could feel his heart pounding as he followed the corridor around, scanning the room numbers.

The door to 122 was ajar, and Truman knocked gently before stepping inside. It was set up like a hotel room more than a hospital room, with carpeting and a dresser and a little desk, the bed neatly made with floral-print pillows.

Sitting in a recliner watching television was an elderly man, definitely not Jaime. He was wearing gray trousers and a plaid shirt and house slippers, and pointed the remote to mute the TV set, looking up at Truman with rheumy eyes.

"Who are you, now?" he asked.

"I'm looking for Jaime Martínez."

"I'm Jamie Martinez," he said, pronouncing the surname as far from the Spanish as technically possible, with the stress on *mar*. "Legally it's James. What's this about?"

It suddenly dawned on him that the nurse hadn't mispronounced Jaime; he really was Jamie, short for James. Truman was the one who'd mangled it.

"Damn it," he said, half to himself.

Jamie laughed. "I'm not who you were expecting. Are you a bill collector, son?"

"I misread the spelling. *Jamie* kind of looks like *Jaime*."

"I get it. My name is Martinez, but I'm about as Hispanic as you are."

"Do you own a liquor store in Westlake?"

"I own the building," Jamie said, "but I sold the business long ago. Before you were allowed to wear long pants."

"Were you ever married to a woman named Catherine Williams?" Truman asked, even though he knew the answer.

"On that count, you've definitely got the wrong guy."

"I'm sorry to have bothered you."

"No bother," Jamie said, gesturing with the remote, his eyes bright. "I don't get many visitors.

You're certainly a strapping young thing."

Truman frowned. "I'm not really that young."

"Compared to me, you are. Did anyone ever tell you that you have great hair?"

"I need to get it cut," Truman said, self-consciously running a hand through it.

"Were you ever in the service? They'd never let you grow it out like that."

"I've always been a civilian."

"That was my job for a while in the Army, cutting guys' hair. It was a great job."

"Interesting," Truman said, shifting his weight impatiently, waiting for the opportunity to excuse himself and leave.

"Don't take this the wrong way, son, but I don't suppose you'd let me touch it."

"My hair?" His eyes narrowed. "Why?"

"For the memories. As you can see, I haven't had my own hair in a long time."

Truman hesitated. It wasn't an appealing proposition. This guy probably had the germs of everyone in the building all over his grubby paws. But he couldn't see any real harm in it either. "Sure," he said finally, and dropped to one knee beside the recliner, tilting his head toward Jamie.

With a sigh, the old man gently touched his head, his hand trembling as it ran through Truman's hair. Truman closed his eyes. He needed to shower tonight anyway. It was a little weird, letting a perfect stranger ruffle it, but the guy was very gentle, and he let it happen. Hearing him grunt, Truman opened his eyes again. There were tears in Jamie's eyes.

"Such a lovely young man," Jamie said softly.

Truman realized then that he'd totally misread the situation. But he held Jamie's gaze, felt the sadness in his eyes. On impulse he leaned in to kiss him. Jamie's mouth was firm and warm, which was surprising, considering his age. He felt Jamie's palm lightly grasp the back of his neck. The old coot was pretty good at this. Truman put a hand on his thigh and slid it slowly toward his crotch. Pulling out of the kiss, Jamie gasped, then pressed his cheek to Truman's, breathing hard, his breath warm on Truman's ear.

At that moment there was a soft knock at the door, and Truman quickly pulled away, tumbling back onto his butt.

"I heard you had a visitor," a woman's voice said. As she stepped in, Truman saw that she was staff, wearing scrubs. Seeing Truman sprawled on the floor, her brow furrowed. "What's going on?"

"Leave us alone, woman," Jamie roared.

"We're just talking," Truman said, getting to his feet, feeling his face burning.

"That's not what it looked like to me," she said sharply. "Jamie, are you OK?"

"Why do I get no privacy here?" he demanded.

"I was having a moment."

"I have to go," Truman said. "It was nice to meet you, Jamie."

"I thought you were a relative," the nurse called after him.

Truman didn't pause to respond, pulling his backpack straps tight and hustling out to the street.

Looking over his shoulder when he was half a block away, he saw that no one was following him, or even watching him leave. That was a relief. Slowing his pace, he took a few deep breaths to slow his racing pulse.

The only option had been to bolt. Those nurses might have tried to pop Truman for trespassing or elder abuse or lewd conduct with a veteran. How stupid was that, not even noticing how the guy's name was spelled, and walking into a seniors residence expecting to find Grant's brother-in-law? He hadn't clued in that Jamie had a hair fetish either, if that's what had just happened. Maybe he wasn't really cut out to be a detective.

FOUR

Once he'd boarded the bus, he checked the route and realized he'd be going right through the Arts District. He texted Celeste:

Still at work? Can I drop by?

Celeste looked at her phone when it buzzed, grinning at Truman's message.

Here till 6. Gallery as crowded as ever.

After she sent it, Celeste glanced around the empty space. The boss wasn't even here today, and the place was positively funereal. Tired of reading, she considered doing some actual work, punching up some of the artists' bios and printing out new copies. But no one was looking at the art in here anyway, so that seemed less than futile.

Digging in her pocket, she found a flat little tablet—Ritalin. But it was almost closing time. If she took it now, it would keep her up too late. Deeper in the pocket she exchanged it for a Vicodin, cracking it between her teeth and chewing it up thoroughly, grimacing at the bitterness, then taking a drink of her coffee to wash away the taste.

Soon the front door swung open, and Truman came in, looking a little warm from his walk from the bus stop.

Glancing up at the mezzanine railing, he saw that the owner's office was dark.

"Have you been alone all day?" Truman said. "How do you stand it? It's so boring."

"It's not that bad. There were some lookie-loos in earlier. We can't all be freewheeling detectives."

Truman sat in the chair in front of her desk and told her about Jamie.

"You kissed him?" Celeste demanded, incredulous. "Truman, you weirdo. I can't even imagine what that was like."

"He was actually a pretty good kisser."

"But he must have tasted like mothballs."

Truman pursed his lips, considering it. "More like butterscotch."

Celeste laughed at that. "Still, you assaulted a defenseless elder."

He threw up his hands. "He wanted it."

"That's what rapists always say," she said emphatically.

"Stop it," Truman protested. "He basically assaulted me."

"It doesn't matter. If he has dementia or Alzheimer's or something, he can't give consent."

"Oh, my god," Truman said, his eyes growing wide. "I molested a veteran."

"But it was really just a kiss, right?"

"I also touched his weenie."

With that Celeste cracked up, giggling uncontrollably, and soon Truman was laughing too.

Feeling his phone buzz in his pants, Truman stood up and pulled it out, quickly regaining his composure. "It's Grant."

"You should answer it," she said.

Truman did, and told him, "I don't have anything to report yet."

"I'm glad you picked up," Grant said. "I've been thinking about you all day. Do you want to get a drink?"

"Can I bring Celeste?"

"Your girlfriend? Sure, why not? Swing by my house. There are lots of fun places around my neighborhood."

"Give me an hour," Truman said, and ended the call. He asked Celeste, "Do you have time for drinks?"

"As long as there's food. Are you inviting me because the metro doesn't go there?"

"Sweetie, you know I love you for more than your car."

"Let me lock up the offices," she said. "Then we can go."

After trotting up the stairs and back down again, she locked the front entrance, set the alarm, and herded Truman out the back door, slamming it firmly and locking the bolt. Her little blue two-door was parked in the alley, and they climbed in, soon nosing into the traffic and heading west.

Pulling up in front of Grant's, Celeste said, "I thought it would be swankier."

"You wouldn't believe what this place is worth," Truman said, climbing out.

Grant met them at the door, stepping outside and greeting them with a smile as he pulled on a sleek leather jacket. He led them down the block to a trendy bar on Sunset, decorated in polished wood and house plants and retro Formica. It wasn't busy yet, and there was room for all three of them to sit at the bar, Grant and Truman on either side of Celeste.

Grant asked for a beer, and Celeste ordered what they usually had, a gin and tonic for her and a margarita for Truman, adding, "Bring me a plate of jibs with that."

"Memphis-style, or Lowcountry?" the bartender asked.

"Whichever's spicier."

"You got it," she said, and stepped away.

"What the hell are jibs?" Grant demanded, frowning.

"It's right there on the chalkboard," Celeste said, pointing it out.

"That doesn't answer my question."

"They're like ribs, but made with jackfruit," she said. "And not just here. It's a thing."

"I guess I need to get out more," Grant said.

Watching them talk, Truman realized that Grant really was concerned about it, seemed worried about being out of the loop. Fleeting bar-food trends were trivial by definition, but if part of his identity was based on knowing such things, it made sense that it would cause him concern. Still, that status-anxiety stuff was more common among clotheshorse types. Grant was well put together, but he didn't read like a fashion victim.

When their round came, Grant set a C-note on the bar, waving dismissively when Truman offered a credit card.

"You said there was nothing to report," Grant said, after he'd clinked his bottle of Corona against each of their glasses, "but have you come up with anything at all?"

"In a way," Truman said, licking the margarita salt from his lips. "I've eliminated a couple of possibilities, and I have an address to hit up tomorrow."

"Where?" Grant said intently, holding his gaze.

"Westlake. Let me look into it first."

Grant nodded and looked away, his demeanor softening again. The bartender set Celeste's plate of jibs in front of her, and she picked one up with her fingers.

"Help yourselves," she said.

"No thanks," Grant said flatly, eyeing the plate. "So Celeste is a heavy-duty Hispanic name. Do you have a nickname?"

"I think it's easy enough to pronounce that Anglos don't usually insist on trampling it," she said. "The worst they can do is drop the *tay*, and that makes it a totally English name." She gestured with a piece of jackfruit. "Truman tried calling me 'Tay' once, until I slapped some sense into him."

"She didn't really slap me," Truman said, leaning forward to look at Grant, frowning and shaking his head. "But it was made clear to me that day that lo—I wasn't to use that name again."

Celeste turned to Grant. "So one of my uncles is trying to sell his house by FSBO," she said, pronouncing it *fizz-bo*. "Do you think that's a bad idea?"

"Fizz-bo," Grant said, and frowned thoughtfully. "You know, I can't really say. I don't deal with their listings. My stuff is more high-end. Luxury properties. The Westside and WeHo."

"Of course," Celeste said, studying him. "You probably don't sell many houses in Boyle Heights."

Grant laughed and slid off his stool. "I'll be right back."

Once he was out of earshot, Celeste said quietly, "He's deflecting."

"What are you talking about?" Truman said. "He just went to pee."

"He doesn't sell houses anywhere if he doesn't know what FSBO means."

"I don't know what it means either."

"That's no surprise—you're a renter. Anyone who's been even tangentially involved with a real estate transaction would know the term."

"What does it mean?" Truman said, frowning and trying to concentrate. On an empty stomach the tequila had hit him quickly, and he felt a little buzzed.

"It's an acronym. F-S-B-O, for sale by owner. People do it to try to save on real estate fees."

"You're right, that does sound pretty basic."

"So he's not really a real estate agent," she hissed.

Grant returned, lowering himself onto his barstool. "Another round?" he said, lifting his mostly empty bottle.

"I have an early morning," Celeste said, wiping her fingers on a napkin.

"You'll stay, though, Truman? I haven't had dinner."

"There's not much vegan stuff for me here," Truman said, scanning the chalkboard. "Unless you want to share some jibs."

"Hell, no," he said. "We'll find a place nearby that has steamed tofu and brown rice."

"That's not what I eat," Truman said, frowning.

"Stay," Grant said, holding his gaze.

Truman nodded, suppressing a smile. He knew what the end game was. Celeste had been right—Grant wanted to sleep with him.

Once they were out on the sidewalk, Grant stretched his back and said, "Would you like us to walk you back to your car?"

"It's two blocks, and this isn't exactly Skid Row," Celeste said. "I'll be fine."

Truman gave her a brief good-bye hug, and Celeste whispered intently in his ear, "Call me."

Grant and Truman watched her go, then headed in the opposite direction, strolling down into Boystown.

"This neighborhood looks different every time I come here," Truman said, taking in the new shops and pubs.

"Is it getting better, or worse?" Grant asked, eyeing him.

"That's hard to say. It's definitely getting pricier."

In the next block they found a falafel shop, and sat on stools at the side of the space to eat. Grant was focused only on Truman, despite all the guys floating around, lots of whom showed interest in Grant and tried to catch his eye. It was flattering, but it made Truman feel self-conscious, knowing he was the object of his attention.

The moment Truman had finished his falafel and crumpled up the wrapper, Grant said, "Do you want to come over to my place?"

"I want to, but I'm not sure we should mix business with sex. I mean, I'm already working for you."

"Right to the point," Grant said, grinning. "I like that. Honestly, though, I don't think one thing will interfere with the other."

"You're not going to try to weasel out of paying me after?"

"I want to be offended by that," he said, raising his eyebrows, "but I want to see you naked even more."

Truman nodded. "Let's go."

Walking back toward his house, Truman grabbed his hand and interlaced their fingers.

Grant seemed surprised, but went with it, at least for a few minutes, until they were waiting at a light to cross Sunset.

"I'm not a party guy," Truman said. "Are you?"

"You mean meth? We won't need drugs. Just looking at you in those pants is blowing my mind."

Truman glanced at him sidelong. The guy was really good at laying down the mack. Even if he tried hard and wore his most flattering jeans, Truman would never look anywhere near as hot as Grant would when he wasn't even trying.

"So why is this happening now?" Truman said. "Why not the night we met at that Mexican place?"

"I was having dinner with someone. But I made note of your flirtatiousness. And I did give you my phone number."

At the door to his house, Grant punched the code into the keypad, his fingers moving fast, but again he didn't even try to conceal it. Once they were inside, he led Truman into his bedroom, tidy and gray and soulless like the front room.

Moving close to him, Truman put his palms on Grant's chest, feeling the muscles.

"You like that?" Grant said softly.

"You're basically perfect," Truman said. "You could get any guy you want. Why me?"

"You underestimate yourself." Grant put his

hands on Truman's waist, pulling him close, and met his mouth, firm and hot and insistent. Pulling back, he unbuttoned Truman's shirt, then his own. Truman squeezed Grant's crotch through his pants. The guy was already hard.

Soon they were both naked, and Truman ran his hands over Grant's flawless dark skin, marveling at how toned he was.

Grant grabbed his cock. "Do you want to fuck me?" he whispered.

Truman's eyebrows shot up. "Sure."

Producing a condom, Grant ripped it open, then kissed Truman again, massaging his cock until he was rock hard, then rolled it on for him. Truman climbed on top of him, gasping with the intensity of penetrating him. Grant knew what he was doing, guiding him, giving him subtle direction.

After they both came, lying there catching his breath, his legs sprawled across Grant's, Truman said, "I was kind of surprised you wanted to get fucked."

"Because I'm a big guy?" Grant said, turning to look at him. "That's a stereotype."

"Maybe it's because you're a take-charge kind of guy. I assumed you'd want to be the boss in bed."

Grant chuckled. "You never know what people are into."

"That's true. With sex, all bets are off."

"In my business it's risky even to be known as gay."

"In real estate?" Truman said, dubious. "I know tons of gay guys who do that."

"Right," Grant said, shifting position. "I guess I mean Westside buyers. People with money are more conservative than you might think, even in LA."

Truman eyed him. "I guess that rings true."

Shifting closer, Grant folded a knee over Truman's leg. "Do you want me to fuck you this time?"

"I'm afraid that ship has sailed."

"You mean you can't go again?"

"Exactly. I'm not a freaking robot."

Grant chuckled. "I like that expression. It sounds like the Revolutionary War or something. The British evacuating New York Harbor for the last time. 'That ship has sailed, good sir.'"

Truman waved languorously. "Bye, George."

"I'm glad you didn't want to get high. It's way more fun like this."

"Do most of the guys you sleep with want to get high first?" Truman said, frowning. "I find that hard to believe. Like I said before, your body is amazing. No chemical enhancements required."

"I just thought because your friend was on downers tonight, maybe you were into that too."

"Celeste?" he said, turning to look him in the eye. "She's not on drugs."

"I'm surprised you didn't see it. I'd bet money she's on opiates."

"It was the booze," Truman said.

"She only had one gin and tonic. Besides, I noticed it before we even sat down."

"What is it exactly that you think you saw?"

"It's in the eyelids. They move a little slow. I've seen it before—it's opiates."

"No fucking way," Truman said, raising his voice.

"Maybe I'm wrong," Grant said gently, running his palm along Truman's belly. "I know she's your friend."

"If she were a junkie, I'd know."

"Just because she was on downers tonight doesn't mean she's a junkie." He sighed. "I know you're a detective, but sometimes it's hard to see what's right in front of your nose."

Truman scoffed and pulled his arm away.

Sitting up, Grant shifted to the side of the bed. The ardor had worn off, and that magnetic look in Grant's eye had evaporated. It often happened with guys once they'd slept together, and Truman knew it wasn't about him personally. It just meant that this was a hookup, Grant wasn't looking for a boyfriend, and there was no point in staying over.

"Do you want to shower?" Grant said. "You go first."

When Truman got out of the tub and started toweling off, Grant stepped in, cranking the water to a high temperature that quickly filled the bathroom with steam.

Surely the guy wouldn't mind lending him a clean pair of underpants, Truman reasoned, walking back into the bedroom, and pulled open the top drawer of the dresser. This was the socks, he saw, and then froze, catching sight of a handgun, silver and black and deadly, just lying there, peeking out among the balls of fabric. A heater, Biff called it in the *Hard-Nosed Detective* handbook.

It wasn't strange that people had guns, even someone with a vanilla job like real estate, but those things were supposed to be locked up. Gingerly closing the drawer, he pulled open the next one, and found the underwear. The ones he chose were slightly big on him, but they felt great, made of some luxy high-tech fabric.

As he got dressed, Grant came out of the shower, a towel tied around his waist, his scalp and his perfect pecs glistening. He saw Truman to the door and kissed him good-bye.

"I'll look forward to hearing what you find about Jaime."

"I'll call you tomorrow," Truman said, and headed out into the dark.

On the way down to Sunset, he checked the time. It was too late to call Celeste. She'd be asleep already. Sunset had a good late-night bus, and he didn't have to wait long for it. Once he was on board, he put in his earbuds and watched the dark city roll by.

Grant was so matter-of-fact in accusing Celeste of being a doper. He had to be misreading it. That had to be the explanation. But just thinking about it gave him a lump in the pit of his stomach. Maybe there really was something to it. He knew her so well, but he didn't know everything.

———·———

Climbing into bed, Truman opened the *Hard-Nosed Detective* book, reading through Biff Sturgis's techniques for catching people in their own lies. "Fabrications tend to drift with time and pressure," he explained. "A snitch will tell you he had ham and eggs at eight before he left his flophouse, and the next day he'll tell you he ate at nine. Slap him around a little and he might have eaten flapjacks. The truth, on the other hand, never changes, no matter what angle you look at it from, no matter how much you sweat the witness."

Later, in the night, Truman woke to the sound of rain on his windows. He watched for a minute, the water spotting and trickling down the tattersall panes. It was comforting, somehow, even though it had interrupted his sleep. Turning over, he soon drifted off again.

FIVE

The rain was past, the sun bright outside when Truman woke to the smell of coffee. Halfway through his first cup, when he looked at his phone, he saw that Celeste had texted:

I want details. Come over here and buy me lunch.

Grinning, Truman texted back:

See you at 1.

Thinking about it, he added:

If I'm the entertainment, you're buying.

A dark shirt and jeans, he decided. Adjusting his hair in the bathroom mirror, he wondered about asking Celeste whether she was on opiates.

A question like that could really come across as an attack. Not today—he needed to think about it first.

After he pulled on a jacket and locked up his pad, he trotted down the stairs for the half-hour walk to Celeste's gallery. When he went in, he saw that the space was abandoned, as always, making the artworks look more dramatic and stark in the big room. Upstairs, the owner's office light was on.

Celeste rose when he came in and called up to the offices. "Saffron? I'll be back in an hour."

She waited to hear a faint "Bye," then stepped out onto the street with Truman.

"Can she hear the door from up there?" Truman asked.

"It won't matter," Celeste said, waving her arm. "No one ever comes in."

They walked to a bistro a couple of blocks away and got seated at a window overlooking a gravel courtyard. The place felt busy, considering it was Monday and the Arts District was more about the weekend. When the waitress swung by, Celeste ordered coffee and a sandwich, and Truman asked for the chopped salad.

"So you went to eat after I left?" Celeste said.

"I guess we did, yeah," Truman said, frowning thoughtfully.

"You don't remember?" she said, incredulous.

"I knew it. You slept with him. He was totally macking on you. Why would you do that when he's so shady?"

"It just kind of happened."

"He's lying about his job," she said. "I thought that might dissuade you in terms of climbing into his bed. What does he really do?"

Truman paused while the waitress set down their coffees, then took a sip before he continued. "It has to be something embarrassing, or something illegal, right? Grant is status-oriented, so if it was something embarrassing, it would have to be low-paying or blue-collar."

Celeste frowned at him over the rim of her cup. "He's not digging ditches or slinging hash, Truman. He's got money."

"He appears to. It doesn't mean he has lots of it. My neighbor works less than I do and drives a Bimmer. Maybe Grant is just stretched a little thin."

"You've lost all objectivity," she said. "That's what happens when you sleep with a guy. Suddenly he can do no wrong."

"I'm just saying we don't know what he does. All we know is that he's lying about it."

"Wake up, man," she insisted. "He paid you a grand in cash before you even did anything. He has to be a gangster or a crook."

"Maybe," Truman said.

"My father uses the catchall term 'lowlife.'"

"Fine," Truman said, and folded his arms. "He's a lowlife."

The waitress set down their food, and Truman tucked into his salad, avoiding Celeste's gaze.

"Are you going to keep working for him?" she said. "Don't you think that might be dangerous?"

"I have to make it look like I'm doing something," Truman said. "That thousand bucks is basically gone."

———◆———

After Celeste paid the check, and hugged him good-bye on the street out front, Truman walked to the metro and rode to Westlake. Following the map on his phone, he was soon walking up on the building Jaime's old landlord had told him about. The faded sign out front confirmed it was the Highland Arms. Taking in the scale of the place, two floors of apartments arrayed around the courtyard, he realized he hadn't really thought this through. Was he going to knock on every door until he found a buxom woman who recognized Jaime's name?

The place was protected by a fence of black steel bars spaced a few inches apart, and the gate was locked, so he couldn't even get inside. But soon after he'd stopped to look through the barrier, a pair of teenagers trotted down the stairs at the left side, talking animatedly, and pushed through the gate. They ignored Truman, allowing him to catch it before it swung closed. He quickly stepped through.

The courtyard had some planter boxes around the sides. The only sign of life was a woman standing at one of them, watering the geraniums with a sprayer attached to a garden hose. Her head was wrapped in a scarf with wispy gray curls peeking out around the edges. Black women usually put a lot of effort into their hair, so seeing the scarf, along with the fact that she was wearing a pink floral housecoat and slippers, he knew she wasn't prepared for visitors. Truman waffled on approaching her, but she noticed his lingering presence, and cut off the spray nozzle, turning to look at him.

"Pardon me," Truman said. "Do you know where the manager is?"

"That's me," she said, and set the hose down on the planter. As he stepped closer, she pulled her coat tighter, and with watery eyes gave him the once-over.

"I'm looking for a guy who might have lived here, or hung around with one of the tenants. His name is Jaime Martínez."

"I don't know anyone like that," she said, her gaze unwavering.

"He has a little scar on his forehead," Truman said, tapping above his eye with his finger.

"Maybe a mustache. Tall and thin."

"It's strange," she said, raising her eyebrows, "to live in a time when so much information is available for free. People forget the old ways. There was a time when you had to work for things, and information was monetized."

Truman frowned. "You want to sell me information about Jaime?"

"Of course not," she said, and scowled. "But a small gratuity might spark my memory. I'm on a fixed income. The owner knocks a few dollars off my rent in exchange for me keeping an eye on this place, but otherwise it's just Social Security for me."

"Fine," Truman said, and dug out a fin, holding it out to her.

"Are you kidding me, son?"

"I'm not psychic," he said, dropping his hand. "Tell me how much you want."

The woman slowly looked behind her into the courtyard, her shoulders rotating with her stiff neck. Truman followed her gaze; there was no one around.

"Let me show you the right way to offer someone a gratuity. Give me the five."

She took the bill and deftly folded it up, then tucked it under her thumb in her right hand.

"Can you see it?" she said, holding out her hand, palm down.

"I can't."

"You will if I want you to," she said, and twisted her wrist, flashing the fin without moving it, giving him a glimpse of the stylized green 5 on the corner of the bill. "Could you see what it was?"

"Cash money."

"And there's no mistaking the denomination." She smiled. "Now take it from me as you shake my hand."

Truman reached for her palm with his fingers, miming a handshake, and took the bill.

"Don't look at it," she admonished him. "You already know what it is. Just pocket it, and no one else can see what transpired."

"Very slick," Truman said, eyeing her appreciatively. It was the kind of skill Biff Sturgis would use. From the lines on her face, this woman was old enough that she could have been his contemporary.

"Now try it with me."

He palmed the five and extended his hand, flashing it to her. With a delicate touch, it was gone, and both her hands rested in the pockets of her housecoat.

"You get the picture," she said. "Now let's try it with one of those other presidents. How about Mr. Jackson? I like the looks of him. He's got a haircut like yours."

"That works," Truman said, and grinned, finding a twenty in his pants and folding it up.

"Do it so that I'll be able to see the number," she said. "You can't negotiate with someone unless you establish clear terms."

After he refolded it to make the 20 visible, he hid it in his palm, then flashed it to her.

"Very subtle," she said, nodding in approval. "You're a natural." Tapping his hand, she made the bill disappear, joining the fin in the pocket of her coat.

"The Mexican with the scar used to visit Norma in 208," she said, gesturing across the courtyard with her chin. "Up the stairs on the left side." She turned to pick up the hose.

The transaction was over, he realized, hesitating momentarily at the sudden shift. He probably shouldn't ask for the sample five back.

"Thank you," Truman said.

"Mm-hmm," she said, not looking at him again.

Heading toward the stairs, he found 208 was the first apartment at the top, closest to the street. When he rang, he heard movement inside, and a woman soon pulled open the inner door, leaving the screen between them. She had Latin features, dark hair with blond highlights, tight jeans, and hefty breasts. This was definitely the woman the guy had described. Norma, the manager had said.

"I'm looking for a guy named Jaime Martínez," Truman said.

She spoke in a thick Spanish accent. "I don't know that name."

But she did—Truman could tell from the flash of concern in her eyes, which she quickly quelled, blinking and shifting to a passive expression.

"Are you sure?" he said. "Several people have linked him to this apartment. He's got a little scar over his eye, and maybe a mustache. He drives a classic muscle car. A Road Runner."

Her eyes narrowed and she stepped closer to the screen. "Who are you?"

"Someone who doesn't want to make a scene in front of your door," Truman said, channeling Biff Sturgis. "Sing, sister."

Norma lowered her voice. "Jaime lived in my spare room for a while. Don't tell the landlord," she said, and tapped a finger to her lips. "But he went back to Honduras. Someone died. Maybe his father. He said he'd come back, but I haven't seen him for months. It's hard to get back across the border."

"You could have told me that first," Truman said irritably. "Do you have a phone number for him?"

She shook her head.

"How about his friends, do you know any of them?"

"He was just a tenant. Sorry."

"Did you ever meet his wife?"

Her eyebrows shot up. "Wife? He doesn't have a wife."

Truman watched her for a moment. Had her accent just slipped?

"Who told you he was married?" she demanded.

Something else was going on, he realized. No way was he going to explain his quest, or mention Grant. Don't reveal what you know—that seemed like a sensible tactic for a detective. It came up when he was conducting tours. One of the seasoned old guides had explained it to him. *When the client is interested in the place, they'll ask—let them lead you.*

"Thanks for your time," Truman said, and went back to the stairs. A moment later, behind him, he heard Norma slam her door.

The sun was on the stairs, and they looked dry after last night's rain, so Truman sat down, a few steps from the top, and pulled out his notepad. No one was around, and the concrete was pleasantly warm. Across the top of a fresh page he wrote NORMA in block letters.

Her story didn't add up, he thought, jotting down what she'd told him. Jaime's landlord said she was a girlfriend, but Norma said Jaime was just a tenant. So why had she reacted to the idea of the guy being married? And no way was he undocumented and sneaking in and out of the country—Grant was established and had resources, and marrying his sister would quickly sort out anyone's immigration issues. Maybe it was a completely different Jaime, like his confusion over elderly Jamie with the hair thing. No, he decided, it was the right guy—the manager had twigged to the scar over his eye.

Above him, then, he heard Norma's voice, and turned to look. Her door was still closed, but the window beside it was open a few inches, covered by a sheer curtain. She was on the phone, he realized, and he was only hearing her side of the conversation. Most interesting of all was that her accent had completely evaporated.

"It's me," she said. "Someone just knocked on my door asking for you…. A stupid-looking white guy, wearing a backpack, like he just got expelled from junior college."

Truman could feel his face heating up. She was one to talk about working a look, with that car-wreck of a dye job, and a bra that was at least a size too small. But putting that aside, this was huge—she was talking to Jaime.

"I didn't tell him anything," she went on. "He didn't know who I was, and he thought you had a wife. Crazy, right?… I don't think so…. He didn't look like one of his guys, but you never know.…

You can't come here. If they know about me, they might be watching for you.... I'll swing by the Stallion.... Love you, *jefe*."

Truman stood up and trod gingerly down the stairs, careful not to make a sound. The manager had disappeared, her watering hose neatly coiled on a hook on the wall. Once he was out on the street he took a breath and stuffed his notepad into his bag. No way was Jaime in Honduras; he was right here in town—and he was hiding from someone. Was he afraid of Grant? That guy had lied about his job, so maybe he'd lied about who Jaime was to him. There were more unknowns than there were answers. But in the bigger picture, he reminded himself, he was making progress—maybe this really was a career that he could handle. That thought made him smile, made the ground feel lighter under his feet.

There'd be a coffeehouse on Wilshire, Truman knew, and he headed that way. When he found a place, he went in and ordered an espresso, carrying the cup and saucer to sit over by the window. After he spritzed the strip of lemon rind into it and had taken a satisfying sip, he pulled out his phone and searched the map for "stallion."

A couple of hotels bore that name, as did a horse-tack business out in the Valley. But the most likely candidate was right here in Westlake—a bar that was just a few minutes' walk.

After he'd planned the route, he drained his cup and headed out. The place looked seedy, at least from the street, with a worn sign above the door, STALLION in curving white script on black. If it was just a dive bar, Truman might be able to pass as a customer, but if it was an immigrant Latin bar, he would definitely stand out. In those places, straight guys competed for straight women, dancing in duple time to that accordion-heavy *norteño* music. This neighborhood was heavily immigrant, so it was totally possible the Stallion was that kind of place.

Truman kept walking. Even if he didn't look like a tourist, Norma said she was coming here, and she already knew what he looked like—and seeing him would spook her.

Circling the block, he headed back to the metro. Once he was on the crowded late-afternoon train, he texted Celeste, maintaining his balance in the moving car by holding the pole in one hand, typing with a thumb on his phone in the other:

New developments. Swing by after work.

Celeste's reply was terse:

Only if you have food.

Truman wasn't about to start cooking, but he could find something on the way home. He had to change trains anyway, and he climbed up out of the earth at Seventh Street, into the Financial District. Within a block he'd found a Cali-fresh place, with mass-produced lunch fare for all the office drones, and bought two burritos.

At home, Truman stretched out on the sofa that faced the windows, digging online for reviews or mentions of the Stallion bar. It didn't seem to be the kind of place that got name-checked or photographed a lot. When the buzzer sounded, he rose and pressed the button to unlock the front door downstairs, then flipped open the deadbolt and went to the counter beside the sink to fetch the burritos.

"You look tired," he said, assessing Celeste when she came in.

"I just worked a full day," she said irritably. "What do you expect?"

"I'm not a scientist, but I'd say you're hangry." He handed her a burrito and followed her to the sofas.

Once she'd peeled open the foil and taken a bite, comfortably installed on the purple sofa, she said, "So what are the developments that required a meeting?"

Between mouthfuls of rice and avocado and black beans, Truman told her about tracking down Norma, and overhearing her phone call to Jaime.

"You did it," she said, grinning at him. "You found the guy."

"He's not staying with her, though. The manager talked like he'd been there in the past, and then Norma told him not to come around."

"But maybe it's close enough. Phone Grant and give him the address, and wash your hands of it."

"If Jaime isn't living there, I haven't really found him."

Celeste balled up her burrito wrapper and threw it overhand toward the kitchen sink, where it bounced onto the counter. "You don't think Norma's address and the name of that bar should be enough for Grant?"

"I could let it go at that, but it doesn't seem very professional."

"You want to be a full-service detective."

"Or at least a thorough detective. I'm thinking the next step is to hang out at the Stallion bar and watch for Jaime."

"You can't," she said flatly. "Norma knows what you look like, and she's already demonstrated that she's not going to give you access to the guy."

"That's why you'd do it," Truman said, holding her gaze.

"Are you kidding me? I'm not going to get involved in this. It's a quagmire, and these people are lowlifes."

"That's why I'd pay you. Grant paid me for two days' work, which I've done, so there's more money coming from him. He's expecting that. It's such a great lead, and I'll make it worth your while. All you'd have to do is hang out and eavesdrop on them. With any luck, you'll get some idea about where he's working, or where he's crashing."

Celeste pursed her lips, considering that. "I have to admit, it does sound like an adventure."

"Right," Truman said emphatically. "You're way more into adventurous stuff than I am. You love Halloween haunted houses, and hiking in the desert, and that channel with the tagline 'television to scare women.'"

"It's 'television to inspire women,'" she said, and frowned.

"Most of the programming is about violent husbands and boyfriends, though."

She folded her arms. "You're not helping to convince me."

"The bar won't be like that. Think upbeat fun, like a roller coaster."

"On a roller coaster, you don't get hit on by drunk vaqueros."

"You can handle that."

She sighed. It was true, she usually could. "I assume you want to do this tonight?"

"Ideally, yeah," Truman said, sitting forward

on the sofa. "Norma said she was going to the Stallion."

"Even the name of it is sleazy. That whole neighborhood—Westlake is just so gross."

"At one time it was the city's wealthiest district. There were Victorian mansions on the hilltops, and tony apartments for the film industry elite."

"It's not like that now, tour guide," she said. "It's fast food and razor wire."

"I can come with you. Maybe I could wait in the car while you go in?"

"There's no point in that." She rose, absently brushing crumbs off her skirt. "I'll have to go home and change first. Where is this place, exactly?"

Truman gave her the address, waiting as she typed it into her phone, then added, "Don't dress too slutty. That'll just call attention to yourself."

"Thanks for that invaluable advice," she said, her brow furrowing. "It's so refreshing to get the male perspective. That never happens."

"I'm not trying to man-splain," Truman said. "You know what I mean."

"I'll call you later," she said, and pulled open the door.

After she'd gone, Truman grabbed one of the Italian sodas from the fridge and dropped onto the purple sofa. He'd hit Grant up for money later, he decided. In person, not by text. Still, he owed him a call. Truman texted him:

> Following up on a lead tonight. More info tomorrow.

SIX

An hour later, Celeste was ready, walking out of her house and climbing into her car. Truman had been vague on whether the Stallion really was a vaquero place or just a dive bar, so she'd done her makeup for somewhere between the two—her eyebrows drawn more severely than she'd wear to an upscale Anglo place, a shade of lipstick darker than she'd ever wear to work, and her hair sprayed and styled. She accessorized her black jeans and a billowy print top with a sparkly little handbag, covered in mirrored sequins. The bag never had anything in it—her keys and cards and phone were safely in her pockets, so if it got stolen, all she'd lose was the accessory itself. Walking around alone in sleazy Westlake, getting mugged didn't seem far-fetched at all.

Starting the car, she paused to dig in the center console, finding a flat little pill and examining it to make sure it was the one she was looking for. It was, she saw, holding it under the light—Ritalin would sharpen things up. Chewing it, the tablet was silky smooth and had no bitterness, tasting of nothing at all.

It took a few minutes to find a parking spot near the bar, and she drove past it twice in her quest. Truman was right; from the outside it was hard to tell what kind of place it was, with just a sign and a heavy door.

Finally she found a street space in front of a well-lit corner store, and deftly backed in, killing the engine. With a deep breath she braced herself as she walked up on the Stallion, then heaved open the door and stepped inside. The place wasn't very big, with some stools at the bar, a trio of booths at one side, and a few tables. Mirrors ran along one wall, and a colorful mural, a stylized rendition of the Aztec calendar with the sun deity grimacing at the center, stretched the length of the room above the booths. In an instant she saw that it was just a run-of-the-mill dive bar, unrenovated since the last century. That was a relief—drunken vaqueros and *norteño* music would have been a lot more work.

Glancing around at the clientele, there were

a pair of college-age women in a booth drinking beer, a straight couple at a table, and a solitary gray-haired guy slouched at one end of the bar. But the sight that made her heart pound was the woman sitting alone at the bar. When Celeste stepped in the door, the woman glanced up with a flicker of interest. She was waiting for someone, but it wasn't Celeste—her eyes went dead, and she looked away. Tight pants, blond highlights, and massive cleavage—this had to be Norma.

The bartender, wearing a baggy gray shirt and a week's stubble, nodded a greeting as Celeste perched on a red vinyl stool a few seats down from Norma.

"Corona," Celeste said, and set her empty handbag on the bar. She had to grin to herself when the guy brought the bottle, setting a lime wedge beside it on the paper coaster: the price he cited was half what it would cost in the places she and Truman usually went to. She found a saw-buck and set it on the bar, sipping at the beer as he took it to the register and made change.

The Ritalin was starting to kick in, making the edges of everything feel a little sharper, the taste of the beer a little more interesting. It didn't really impair perception or cognition; it was more like an enhancement. She didn't do it because she wanted to change things, she told herself, just to brighten things up, make reality more vivid.

As subtly as she could, she checked out Norma, eyeing her sidelong. Norma sat with her elbows straddling a lowball glass on the bar. She looked bored.

The plan Celeste had when she'd come in here was just to watch and listen. But there was no sign of Jaime, and Norma wasn't talking to anyone else. Maybe there was another way. Norma looked tough, she decided, but that didn't necessarily mean she'd subject Celeste to a beat-down. Even if it came to that, the bartender looked competent, and he would probably intervene.

Setting down her bottle, Celeste waved the bartender over.

"Do you know a guy named Jaime Martínez?" she asked, loud enough to be overheard. "I know he comes in here. Skinny guy, mustache. He's got a little white scar on his forehead."

The bartender's eyes flicked to Norma, but then he caught himself. "Doesn't sound familiar," he said firmly, and stepped away.

Celeste took another sip, feeling the heat of Norma's burning glare like a sunlamp on her cheek. Ignoring her, she took the lime wedge that had come with her beer and pressed it into the neck of the bottle. Finally Norma spoke.

"Why are you looking for Jaime?" she demanded, leaning toward her.

"Do you know him?" Celeste said innocently,

turning to meet her gaze.

"Maybe. Who's asking?"

"I know this is his place," Celeste said, and smiled. "I thought I might run into him."

"That fucking prick," Norma snapped.

"Oh, god," Celeste said, feeling her face redden. "Are you with him or something?"

Norma stared at her for a moment before she answered. "You know, I don't think I am."

"I'm going to go," Celeste said, and reached for her change. "Coming here was stupid."

"Don't bother," Norma said, and stepped off her stool. "I'm the one who's going."

"Listen," Celeste said, feeling a twinge of guilt. "Nothing happened between me and him. Maybe it's not even the same guy."

"It's him," she said, and pushed her hair back. "I can't tell you how many times he cheated on me." She looked Celeste up and down. "Usually it's with women who look way trashier than you. I don't think he's even capable of loving a human being. Only that goddamn car."

"I didn't know any of this."

"Of course you didn't. Why would he tell you? He's a sleazeball." Her face twisted into a sad smile. "But I always took him back. What does that say about me? I'm the stupid one."

"I didn't come in here to mess up your love life," Celeste said, wincing at the emotion contorting Norma's face.

Norma's eyes went hard. "You don't need to worry about me. If you do get with Jaime, you're only going to be messing up your own life." With that, she left.

"Damn it," Celeste muttered, twisting on her stool to watch her walk out. It would have been easier if Norma had been angry with her. Slinging vague fabricated innuendo about a guy she'd never met—hurting Norma that way was so much worse.

The bartender stepped over and picked up the single Norma had left for him on the bar top, his brow furrowing as he glanced around the room, ignoring Celeste. He must not have seen Norma leave. That made sense, she realized—he'd been over at one of the booths flirting with the women sitting there, so he hadn't overheard her conversation with Norma.

She dug in her pocket for a Vicodin, popping the whole tablet in her mouth and then washing it down with beer. That ought to even things out. Glancing absently at her phone, she wondered whether she should text Truman. To hell with him—this was all basically his fault. Doing his bidding, she'd messed up someone else's relationship. Jaime was probably on his way here to meet Norma right now. Celeste had to try to talk to him, she decided. Otherwise what she'd just done to Norma had no point, was nothing more than trashy and cruel.

Before she'd even set her bottle down, Jaime walked in, recognizable by his wiry frame and little mustache, his identity made unmistakable by the small white mark above his eye. Dark and with high cheekbones, he looked like some of Celeste's mother's people, who came from the ranchos of Zacatecas and Durango. Greeting the bartender, Jaime sat a couple of stools away, where Norma had been.

"Whatever's on tap," he said, and when the bartender came back with a pint glass, Jaime handed him a twenty and asked, "Has Norma been around?"

"She left a few minutes ago," he said as he turned to the register.

"Seriously?" Jaime said, raising his voice and frowning at the guy's back. "I'm, like, twenty minutes late."

Celeste leaned toward him. "I think it's about more than your timing."

"You talked to her?" Jaime said, meeting her gaze.

"Briefly."

"What was she mad about?"

"Some kind of man trouble," Celeste said, trying to sound casual.

"Oh, god. What did I do now?"

She shrugged. "I didn't get all the details."

Jaime huffed and pulled out his phone.

"I wouldn't do that, fella," she said.

Jaime looked at her again. "How do you know what I'm doing?"

Because men are simple, she thought, but didn't say that. Instead, she said, "You're going to call her, and ask her what's wrong, and tell her it's all a misunderstanding."

His eyebrows shot up. "Good guess. Why shouldn't I do that?"

"She knows," Celeste said pointedly, then picked up her beer.

"About the girl with the tats? That was nothing. I slept with her, like, twice." Jaime looked at his phone, but hesitated.

"A woman needs time to cool off," Celeste said. "Give her some space."

"You think?" he said, frowning.

"Trust me—I know."

Jaime set his phone on the bar, then shifted gears, subtly checking out Celeste's body as he gulped at his beer.

"Have you been together long?" she asked.

Jaime looked away but said, "Yeah."

"It can't be that serious. I don't see a ring on that finger."

"You're not shy," he said, and chuckled. "What's your name?"

"Penelope."

"I don't meet many Latinas with that kind of handle."

"My parents wanted to mainstream me," she said, gesturing vaguely. "You know how it is."

"Sure I do," he said, and flashed a smile.

It was dazzling, that expression, and made it hard to think clearly. The guy must know it had that kind of power. No matter how charming he was, she reminded herself, he was still a cad—a self-professed one, even. But she listened to him talk, trying to be clever in her responses without being too flirty, and gradually built the connection.

"So where's your boyfriend?" Jaime said finally, sipping at his glass.

She stretched her arm out and spread her palm. "In a direction I can't point."

"He's in lockup?"

Celeste laughed. "I meant somewhere in the future."

He nodded approvingly and reached for his phone. "Let me get your number, girl."

"Only if you give me yours, boy."

Jaime grinned and recited it, and Celeste typed it into her phone, then sent him a text:

Penelope

"Now you have mine," she said, seeing it flicker

on his screen. "So are you actually going to call me, or are you just shooting the breeze?"

"I'll call," he said, and winked at her.

Celeste picked up her change, leaving a dollar for the bartender, and slid off her stool. "Don't wait too long," she said, and held Jaime's gaze just long enough to remove all ambiguity.

Walking out, she felt him watching her, checking out her figure. She didn't mind the feeling at all.

On the street she headed for the corner store, still open and brightly lit. Pausing to look back to make sure she was alone, she climbed into her car and felt around in the console until she found a Vicodin, then snapped half of it off in her teeth. The first one hadn't kicked in yet, and another half wasn't excessive, she told herself.

She needed to talk to Truman, but she didn't want to go back to his place, where there was nothing stronger than Italian soda. Downtown was on the way home, and it was easy for carless Truman to get there. She texted him:

Meet me upstairs at Clifton's.

Climbing the stairs through the faux forest of the cafeteria, she found the bar level wasn't that crowded. The space was vast, with a long bar snaking around the room, and the rough bark of a massive redwood rising out of the middle of the polished floor, as if the room had been built around the tree. Truman wasn't here yet, and she found a spot on a tall chair at the bar, leaning back and setting her handbag in front of her.

The vibe was completely different from the Stallion. Here people were dressed up for a night out, and there were proportionally way more Anglos. The bartender, a woman with a cute little bow tie and a black vest over a white shirt, her hair pulled back tight, stepped over, and Celeste ordered a tonic water.

"Can you put a piece of lime in it?" she said, and the woman nodded, flashing her a smile.

She was feeling the Vicodin now—the world had slowed down a notch, leveled out a little. Booze would only muddle her mind-set, and the buzz was way better without it.

From the other side of the room, a guy with wavy black hair and a pink polo shirt approached.

"Are you drinking alone?" he said, resting a hand on the bar beside her and leaning in, a louche grin on his face.

"I'm waiting for someone," she said firmly.

"Can I keep you company until he gets here?"

Celeste looked him over. He wasn't cross-eyed yet, or slurring his words, but he did seem a little drunk.

"Back off, Jack, or I'll punch you in the throat," she said firmly.

"Whoa." The guy recoiled. "That's a little hostile."

The bartender appeared in front of them. "Your friends are looking for you," she said, and jutted her chin across the room.

The guy threw up his hands as he walked away. The bartender winked at Celeste, then went down the bar. As she returned with Celeste's tonic water, Truman stepped up beside her.

"I'd like a blended margarita," he told the woman, his tone chipper and bouncy.

"Do you care about the tequila?" she asked him.

"Whatever's cheap."

Celeste set a twenty on the counter, but the bartender pushed it back to her. "If he's drinking, that makes you the designated driver. It's on the house."

"Ooh, she likes you," Truman said, once she was gone, and climbed onto the next chair.

"Probably because I'm on tonic water. Sober people are less obnoxious."

"Plus you're cute," Truman said, and reached for her handbag. "Sparkly," he said, and pulled it open.

"That's mine," Celeste protested.

"It's totally empty," he said, holding it open toward her and frowning.

"It's still mine." She sighed and took it from him, then snapped it closed.

"How was the Stallion?"

"No vaqueros," she said, and told him about talking to Norma, and meeting Jaime, pausing while Truman paid for his margarita.

"I can't believe you got his number," Truman said, beaming at her and absently wiping the salt residue off his lip. "That's huge."

"It's your fault that I split them up. You turned me into a mean girl, and I broke her heart."

"I never told you to do that."

"Well, this whole thing is your drama."

Truman sipped at his drink again before he spoke, assessing Celeste. She looked tired. Was that one of the side effects of downers? But she'd worked all day, and had been stalking his target tonight; of course she was tired. He pushed the idea out of his mind.

"It sounds like Jaime was already cheating on her," Truman said. "Plus she threw him over pretty fast. It's like she was planning it, or she was waiting for the right opportunity."

"Maybe."

"So maybe you just accelerated what was already happening with them. Jaime sounds kind of lecherous. Maybe it's not about you at all."

"OK, Truman," she said sharply, waving a hand. "I get it."

Truman watched her quietly for a moment. Why was she so concerned about these people? A few hours ago she'd dismissed them as lowlifes.

"You have to get a date with the guy," Truman said finally. "That way I could talk to him."

"That's up to Jaime. He has to call me—I can't call him."

"I thought you got his number."

"I did, but he has to be the one to make the call."

"That makes no sense."

"You don't get how boy-girl stuff works," she said, and drank from her glass.

"It can't be that different."

"I've seen you pick up a guy just by squinting at him." She lowered the pitch of her voice, mimicking him. "'Hey, man, are you nearsighted, or are you trying to sleep with me?' Straight people have a lot more work to do."

"Most people are straight. It's the default setting. I think it would be a lot easier."

"Trust me, it's not," she said. "Straight guys are animals. Before you came in here, some frat guy was all over me. It's not fun."

"Is he still here?" Truman said, his brow furrowing. "I'll go talk to him."

Celeste scoffed. "I don't need to be defended—I took care of it myself. I need you to listen. I'm not going to call Jaime."

"Got it," Truman said, and lifted his glass to her, then drained it. He didn't quite get why she was upset, but he was smart enough to know not to press it.

"Did you scope out the guys?" he said, glancing around the bar. The booze was starting to hit, making the place more interesting. "Maybe we should be presenting the irresistible dichotomy to eligible bachelors."

"I'm not feeling it," Celeste said.

Hesitating for a moment, he said, "Another round?"

"Let's just go."

Once they were out on the sidewalk, Truman said, "Thanks for doing all this. I'll cut you in once I get some more dough from Grant."

Celeste paused to give him a brief hug before they parted. "I guess as long as I think of it as work, it doesn't seem so crass."

SEVEN

Waking up to the scent of coffee, bright light streaming in the windows, Truman got out of bed and tiptoed across the ice-cold floor to pour a mugful, then climbed back under the covers. Celeste had taken it so personally, the thing with Norma and Jaime. Maybe it had been a mistake bringing her in on this. Biff Sturgis explained how to conduct research using operatives, but he was talking about employees, not friends. Picking up his phone, Truman dialed her number.

"Sorry if I was kind of a dick last night," he said when she picked up.

"I'm used to it. You're always a dick."

"Ouch," Truman said, and laughed.

"I know it's not really my fault. Maybe I did

Norma a favor."

"That's a much better perspective. Listen, do you know anyone who's a real estate agent? While we're waiting for Jaime to call you, I want to find out how severely Grant is messing with me."

"My cousin Marco sells houses," she said.

"Have I met him? You have so damn many cousins."

"He was at my mom's birthday."

"Wait—Marco, the smoking-hot one with the pomp and the nice clothes?"

"That's him," she said.

"Is he gay?"

"You asked me that at the birthday party. He's married to a woman. They've got two little kids running around."

He sighed. "You could have lied to me."

"You know what, Truman?" she said intently. "Marco *is* gay, and he asked about you."

Truman laughed at that, then winced as his mirth sloshed a slug of hot coffee onto his bare belly.

"He works in an office out in Whittier," Celeste said. "It'll be hard for you to go out to meet him, but maybe you could talk on the phone."

"It's actually easy to get to that part of town. There's a commuter train that runs during office hours."

"I'll find out if he's around today," she said, and ended the call.

Truman got up to wipe off the spilled coffee, then pulled on his clothes rather than going back to bed. By the time he was dressed and starting to warm up, his phone buzzed with a text from Celeste:

Marco's in his office. Expecting your visit.

A second message came with the street address. When he looked at it on a map, the navigation software said it was a two-hour walk from the train station. No way was he going to walk that far, but at least he could get most of the way there on the rails.

Pulling on a jacket and his backpack, Truman locked up and walked to the metro, then got on the commuter line at Union Station. From the platform nearest to Marco's office, he called a ride-share, and a few minutes later he was walking into the guy's office, a low industrial building surrounded by acres of parking.

Truman asked for Marco at the front desk, and a moment later a familiar figure stepped out of one of the back offices. Beaming as he called Truman's name, he stepped up and firmly shook his hand.

Marco could have been a model, with his flawless skin, that great haircut, the effortless poise. His suit was flashy, and when he slid his hands into his pants pockets, Truman could see his ample pecs bulging under his shirt. This guy could tell him anything and he'd believe it—he was just too good-looking to challenge, or disbelieve, or even doubt.

Clapping Truman on the shoulder, he led him back to his office and sat behind his desk, waving to the chair in front.

"Celeste said you need a real estate agent," he said, lacing his fingers behind his head and reclining. "You're smart to look in this neighborhood. It's heavily Latin but well integrated. People have real pride of ownership in their properties."

"I'm not actually looking for a house," Truman said, setting his backpack between his feet. "I wanted to ask you about your industry."

"You want to become an agent?" Marco said, raising his eyebrows.

Truman laughed nervously and looked away, feeling himself blushing. He knew he was acting stupid, like he'd never talked to a hot guy before, but he couldn't help himself.

"It's not for me. I'm working a contract for someone who said he's a real estate agent. I'm wondering if you can verify whether he really is or not."

"Agent credentials are public record," Marco

said. "You can look him up yourself. It sounds like you wasted a trip."

"I never even thought to check whether that was possible," Truman said, and sighed. "So is there any chance a guy in your job would not know what a FSBO is?"

"I'd say no—unless he had a concussion, or a stroke, or amnesia, like on TV." He sat up, pulling his keyboard toward him. "What's this guy's name?"

"Grant Williams," Truman said. "He lives in West Hollywood."

"Give me a second." Marco pecked at the keys and studied his screen. "There's nobody in this business with that name around here," he said finally. "An agent in South Florida has that name." He twisted the screen around so that Truman could see it. The image was of a rotund white guy with gray hair, in a suit and tie, smiling for a studio portrait.

"This guy is half that age," Truman said, "and bald, and African American."

"So I'd say your instinct was right," Marco said. "He's not an agent. What kind of work are you doing for him?"

"Some research. Celeste got suspicious when he didn't know about the FSBO thing," Truman said, and stood, swinging his backpack onto his shoulder. "Thanks for your time."

Marco rose and shook his hand again. "I'm sure we'll see you at the next family gathering. So are you dating Celeste?"

"Oh, god, no. We're just friends. We usually wind up chasing the same kind of guys."

Marco laughed at that and saw him to the front door.

Outside, Truman walked through the sea of parking to the street and then to the next corner, out of sight of the real estate office, before he called a ride-share. In the car on the way to the station, he thought about Grant. Why would he lie about something as basic as his job?

On the train he found a quiet place to sit and then phoned Grant, glad that he picked up.

"I wanted to give you a progress report," Truman said.

"Did you find Jaime?"

"I think so. I'm waiting for a call back."

"Excellent. Where is he?"

"In town. I'm not sure where he's staying, but I should know soon."

"I suppose you need more money."

"Eventually, yeah," Truman said. "Let's see what I turn up in the next day or two."

"So you don't need to come to my place for that," Grant said. "But do you want to swing by anyway?"

"To hook up?"

"That was my implication, yes."

"It'll take me about an hour."

"I'll be here," Grant said, and ended the call.

Why had he agreed to go over there with absolutely no hesitation? Truman wondered, watching the concrete and stucco and weeds flash past outside the train window. The guy was hot, but it was probably a bad idea.

———◆———

After she'd set up Truman's meeting with Marco, sitting at her desk in the empty gallery, Celeste got to thinking about tracking down Jaime. She had to wait for him to call, but there was something else she could look into in the meantime.

Tapping at her phone, she dialed Truman.

"Did you talk to Marco yet?" she asked.

"I'm on the train headed out there."

"What kind of car did you say Jaime drove?"

"It's a '72 Road Runner, the guy told me. Matte black. Why?"

"There can't be that many of them around," she said. "I might be able to get some info."

After she ended the call, Celeste got up and walked over to the metal staircase that led up to the mezzanine and the boss's office. Originally it had been utilitarian, this flight of stairs, a way to get from the warehouse floor to the offices upstairs. With the building in its new incarnation as an art space, and after a sandblast cleaning, today these stairs exemplified industrial chic.

Saffron was in today, office lights on and working quietly, a spreadsheet open on her screen. She must have heard Celeste climbing the stairs, because she twisted her chair away from her computer to face the office door. Wearing a gray turtleneck and tight navy pants that accentuated her annoyingly model-thin figure, Saffron must have a meeting later, as her jet-black hair was up in a beehive with neatly feathered bangs. No one would invest that much time on their hair just to sit alone in an office.

It was a carefully cultivated image—the hair, the outfit, the whole gallery. Celeste had no idea where the money came from, whether it was Saffron's or her family's or some silent investor, but funding was coming from somewhere; the sales here in a typical month barely covered the electric bill. Even her name was part of the look she was working—in documents that crossed Celeste's desk, her legal name was Jane. But Saffron fit her, Celeste had to admit, as she had dark South Asian features; no one could accuse her of appropriating someone else's culture. Her surname, Swati, sounded Indian too, so maybe she was just reclaiming her own culture.

"How's it going down there?" Saffron said.

"Do you remember a while back a client who

was in the antique car business?"

"Of course. Her name is Bibi. She wanted three matching canvases in postmodernist style, and they had to have cars in them. I helped her commission the artist."

"I never met her," Celeste said, "but I dealt with that artist, and he mentioned the car thing. Do you have a relationship with Bibi?"

Saffron raised her eyebrows. "Are you in the market for a classic car?"

Celeste chuckled. "I'm not buying. I just wanted to ask her some questions."

"Let me make a call," she said, and swiveled back to her computer screen.

Celeste went down the stairs and sat at her desk, not expecting to hear more about it anytime soon. But a few minutes later, Saffron came down, her spike heels clanking on the bare metal steps.

"Let's go see Bibi," Saffron said, standing there with her keys dangling languorously from her upturned hand.

"Seriously? I thought I could just talk to her on the phone."

"Nonsense. It's an opportunity to network with a client. She invited us over."

Celeste furrowed her brow. "Should I go on my own? I hate to drag you away from work."

"Bibi invited us to her house. Under no circumstances am I going to miss that."

"I guess it won't hurt to close up for a while," Celeste said, and rose, grabbing her sweater.

Saffron went to the front door and flipped the deadbolt, turning over the little sign in the window so that it read CLOSED. "I think it makes the place interesting to be inaccessible in the middle of the day. People walking by will wonder 'What's in there?' It adds to the mystique."

"It also adds zero to the bottom line," Celeste said flatly, following her to the back door and waiting while she set the alarm, then stepped out the fire door into the alley. Saffron's car sat in the parking spot nearest the door, next to Celeste's. The lettering above the grill identified it as a Range Rover, but the thing was smaller than an SUV, styled like it wanted to be a sedan. It was such a bougie ride, but it fit Saffron's image. Even with its stunted proportions it loomed over Celeste's little blue car.

"Can you drive?" Saffron said, handing her the key.

"Are you sure you trust me? This thing looks expensive."

Saffron just laughed and walked around to the passenger door.

Once Celeste had adjusted the seat and the mirrors, she backed into the alley and headed for the street.

"Where are we going?"

"The Bird Streets," Saffron said absently, checking her face in the mirror on the back of the visor.

So this was going to be a time-consuming outing, Celeste realized. That neighborhood was way across town.

The oversize car took more focus to navigate than her own vehicle, and Celeste gripped the wheel tightly as she got used to it, soon accelerating onto the freeway.

"So what does Bibi do in the car market?" Celeste asked.

"Sells them, I think," Saffron said, glancing up from her phone. "She has a couple of garages where they fix up the mechanical bits and repaint them, and then she has a showroom somewhere in the South Bay. People are willing to pay a premium for a classic if it's in good shape."

There must be a lot of people paying a premium, Celeste thought, when they found the driveway to Bibi's house, in the hilly Bird Streets. This was a tony neighborhood. Once she drove through the hedge, they were in a wide courtyard in front of a huge house, a chic gray concrete box with broad windows on two floors. It had to be new—she'd only seen this architectural style in the last few years. At the left was a long garage with half a dozen bays, one of them open to reveal a glimpse of a bright-red open sports car.

"Park by the house," Saffron said, and Celeste swung the car up to the building, tires crunching on the fine gravel.

Saffron flipped down the visor and spent a minute touching up her lipstick. Eventually satisfied, she popped open her door.

Celeste climbed out too and followed her to the front entrance. Painted red, it was actually two doors, together wide enough to drive a truck through. Rather than knock, Saffron just pushed one of them open and walked in.

This was the foyer, Celeste saw, encompassing both floors. A bulky chandelier cascaded overhead, also in simple modernist style; she'd probably recognize the designer's name. A set of floating wooden stairs led upward in a graceful arc. Celeste took it all in, admiring the clean lines and the cavernous space. The things you could do if you had money.

"This way," Saffron said, walking to the back of the space and pushing through a set of glass doors.

Celeste followed her out onto the pool deck, surrounded by a tall hedge on one side and a lush lawn on the other. There wasn't a view from here, even though you expected one in these hillside homes. Instead there was a retaining wall for the neighboring house farther up the hill, and a vista of some treetops at the side. Even without scenery, it was a lovely backyard, and the pool looked inviting, sparkling blue in the sunshine.

"You're here," a woman's voice called, and they both turned to look in the shady space next to the house. Rising from a chaise longue, Bibi came to greet them. In a worn T-shirt and jeans, a ball cap over her short blond hair, she looked ready to change a flat tire or drain a crankcase, not lounge by the pool.

"Lovely to see you," Saffron said, exchanging an air kiss with her.

Turning to Celeste, Bibi shifted her cap higher on her head and looked her over. "Where has Saffron been hiding you?" she asked, her gaze lingering on Celeste's cleavage.

"The name is Celeste," she said, extending a hand. "Thanks for meeting me."

Bibi clasped her hand in both of hers, giving it a warm squeeze. "Do either of you want to take a dip? I've got the heat on in the pool."

"I didn't bring a swimsuit," Celeste said.

"Why would you need one of those?" Bibi said, eyeing her with a wry smile.

"It looks delightful," Saffron said, "but I don't want to mess up my hair."

"Drinks, then? I could make sangria, or margaritas."

"It's broad daylight," Saffron said, frowning and gesturing to the yard. "It'll have to be margaritas."

Bibi stepped back toward the house and slid open a door, revealing a glimpse of a kitchen countertop.

"Lucia," she shouted. "Bring us a pitcher of 'ritas."

Sliding the door shut without waiting for a reply, Bibi grabbed a patio chair and carried it over beside her chaise, then moved another. She was strong for her size, effortlessly heaving up the wrought-iron frames.

"Sit," she commanded, and dropped onto the chaise, pulling off her cap and running a hand through her hair.

It was wise of her to stay in the shade, Celeste thought. With that milky blond complexion, she could pass for an albino, and without sunscreen she'd burn in minutes.

"So you're looking for a classic car," Bibi said, eyeing Celeste. "You'd look great in a convertible, with your hair blowing in the wind."

"You are such a flirt," Celeste said, and laughed.

"She's just being a salesperson," Saffron said, gesturing languidly.

"Oh, no, I'm flirting," Bibi said. "When I meet a beautiful woman, I can't help myself."

"I'm flattered," Celeste said. "But don't you have a girlfriend already?"

Bibi furrowed her brow. "Now, how did you know that?"

Anyone who was so relentlessly on the make all the time probably had several romances to juggle, Celeste thought. Like Jaime, balancing Norma and the woman with the tats, and at the same time hitting on Celeste.

Celeste cocked her head, looking thoughtful. "Anyone with such charming manners and such devastating good looks can't possibly be single."

Bibi cackled, tossing her head back. "Now you're the one blowing smoke. Good for you."

"I wouldn't do that to you, Bibi," Celeste said, holding her gaze. "I get the feeling you don't have a high tolerance for bullshit."

"You're right about that, sister."

"It's a real advantage in business," Saffron said. "Speaking frankly, I mean. You always know where things stand."

The kitchen door slid open, and a woman stepped through carrying a tray with a pitcher and some glasses on it. Curvy and wearing a pink bikini, she couldn't have been more than twenty. Her dark hair was damp, as if she'd already been in the pool.

"Thanks, honey," Bibi said, sitting up and waving for her to set the tray on the foot of the chaise. "This is Lucia."

Bibi poured slushy green margarita into four tumblers while Celeste and Saffron introduced themselves. Lucia murmured in acknowledgment and sat on the chaise longue next to Bibi's.

"Cheers," Bibi said, once they each had a glass, and raised hers.

They were strong—that pitcher must have a whole fifth of tequila in it. Celeste took just a tiny sip. If she had to drive back downtown, there was no point in getting buzzed.

"So—classic cars," Celeste said. "You sell them?"

Bibi nodded. "Find them, fix them, sell them."

"I'm not in the market, but I wanted to ask if you'd ever come across a specific car. It's a '72 Road Runner. Matte black."

"That's a nice vehicle," Bibi said, raising her eyebrows. "Fast. Does it have a manual transmission?"

"I'm not sure."

"I've sold a few of those over the years, but never a matte black one. They didn't do matte finish in the factory. I always try to get the paint job as close to the original as possible. When I'm done with them, they shine like brand-new toys."

"Is there any way to find out who owns a specific classic car?"

"Do you know the VIN or the tag?" Bibi said, raising an eyebrow.

"What's the tag?"

She grinned. "The license plate number."

"I don't have either one."

"There are a few other dealers around," Bibi said, sipping her margarita, "and small shops that do custom jobs, and of course cars change hands privately all the time. I really don't think you'll be able to track it down that way."

"So where did you see this car?" Saffron asked.

"It belongs to a guy I met," Celeste said. "I wondered where he got it."

"Not from me," Bibi said. "Is he a boyfriend?"

"I hardly know him."

"Men are trouble," Bibi said, shaking her head. "And altogether unsatisfying."

Saffron laughed. "That's a pretty broad generalization."

"Maybe," Bibi said. "What does Celeste think?"

"It depends on the guy," Celeste said, and shrugged.

"Stop flirting with her," Lucia demanded, glaring at Bibi.

"Baby, relax," she said, squeezing her knee. "I'm just trying to be a good host."

Lucia scoffed and set her glass on the concrete deck, then heaved herself up and strode over to the pool, diving in with a heavy *splash.*

"So where did you hang the paintings I sold you?" Saffron said.

"They're down at the showroom," Bibi said, and the two of them talked about art for a while, and then business.

Celeste nursed her drink, only half listening to the pair of them talk about people she didn't know, and watched Lucia paddle around in the pool. When Saffron's glass was empty, Celeste caught her eye and tapped her wrist.

Saffron took the hint and rose.

"Good luck tracking down that Road Runner," Bibi said. "Let me know if you ever need a set of wheels yourself."

"I will," Celeste said, and waved to Lucia in the pool as they left.

Once they were back at her car, Saffron said, "I don't think I can drive. What about you?"

"I barely touched that margarita," Celeste said, and went to the driver's side.

"Too bad she didn't have any useful information for you," Saffron said, as Celeste eased the car into the driveway.

"I did learn something, though. That house is so glam—there's definitely money to be made in old cars."

EIGHT

Truman could have taken the bus from the metro to Grant's house, but he wanted time to think, so he walked. As he turned onto Grant's block, he saw that the big red car was parked in the driveway, with the top up. Pulling out his phone as he approached the house, he paused briefly to snap a photo of the vehicle in profile, and then the car's rear end, with the license plate. He had no idea how to look it up, or if that was even possible for anyone besides the police. But it might be, and it might tell him something factual that wasn't subject to Grant's lies.

When he rang the bell, Grant opened the door, flashing that beautiful smile. His shirt was hanging open, revealing his perfect chest.

"You look sweaty," he said, closing the door behind them.

"I've been walking," Truman said.

"Let's get you sweatier."

Truman dropped his backpack on a chair and followed Grant into the bedroom, letting him unbutton his shirt. Kissing him, getting lost in his taut insistent mouth, Truman took hold of his waist and pulled him closer, feeling his raging woody through his pants.

"Fuck me," Grant whispered in his ear.

Once they were naked, Truman pushed him down on the bed, straddling him and relishing the touch of his warm skin. Grant found a condom in the bedside table, and Truman rolled it on himself, pushing up Grant's knees and gasping at the intensity as he entered him. Mouths locked together as Truman built up the rhythm, Grant suddenly twisted his face away, his eyes squeezed shut as he came. The sensation brought Truman to the brink, and after he came, he collapsed on top of him, resting his chin on Grant's thick shoulder, hot and sweaty and sated.

When he'd caught his breath, Truman rolled onto his back.

"That was so freaking hot," Grant said. "So how did you find Jaime?"

"It started with the address you gave me, but I've connected half a dozen other pieces of information since then. It might take another day or so to pin him down."

"Have you found any of his friends or relatives? What information have you got, exactly?"

"I'll put all that in my report," Truman said. "I need a little more time."

"I'd hate to think you were dicking me around."

"You let me fuck you," Truman said sharply, "but you don't trust me to do my job. That's messed up."

Grant chuckled and shifted position, running his hand over Truman's belly. "Relax, hot stuff. I'm just anxious to find Jaime."

"So where is your real estate office?"

"I work freelance. You know, from home."

"I didn't know real estate people could do that."

Grant turned toward him, curiosity in his eyes. "Listen, it took you longer to get here than I expected. I have to go out to a meeting."

Truman sighed. "Which direction are you headed?"

"Downtown. It's on Fig, near that mall."

"Can I get a ride?"

"Of course you can," Grant said, and gently ran his hand over Truman's chest. "If you hustle, you can even shower first."

"I don't need to."

"Right," Grant said, and rolled off the bed.

In reality Truman wanted nothing more than to shower, to wash away the sweat and the funk and the germs, but the opportunity to poke around while Grant was doing that was even more enticing.

As soon as he heard the water running, Truman got up and toweled off, washed his hands in the kitchen sink, and then pulled on his clothes. Treading silently over to the dresser, he gently slid out the sock drawer. The handgun wasn't in sight this time, but when he gingerly felt the jumbled balled-up cotton and polyester, he found its hard mass underneath.

Truman wasn't about to handle the heater, or even touch it, but he had a vague notion that maybe he could take a photo of the serial number and look it up somewhere. Moving the socks out of the way, he pulled out his phone and turned on the flashlight, leaning close to study the ugly metal. There were no numbers on it anywhere, not on the grip or on the barrel. Using a sock to gently flip it over, he studied the other side. Maybe the serial number was on an inside surface, or maybe Grant had scraped it off. There was no point in photographing it without that identifier, he decided, and rearranged the socks to cover it up again.

Stepping out of the master, he went to the

other bedroom, scanning the space from the doorway. Besides a tidily made bed, a night table, and an empty desk against the wall, it was devoid of furniture. The front room had just the boring sofa and chairs and a couple of generic artworks on the walls. He stood with his hands on his hips and surveyed the TV, the credenza, the matching lamps. Even the tchotchkes on the mantel were soulless. The whole place looked like a damn hotel room.

Maybe it was, he realized—maybe Grant was renting this house. The furniture and the art and the lack of anything personal—no photos, no books—implied as much. Why hadn't he thought of that before? There were tons of houses and apartments used for short-term rental. Some of his tour clients had told him horror stories about getting off the plane from Germany or Australia, amped up for a vacation, and moving into a place with dirty sheets and towels, used syringes in the garbage, duct tape holding cracked windows together. But this place was a lot nicer than that. If it was a rental, it was in a completely different category.

There was some food here, he saw, looking in the fridge and then opening a couple of the kitchen cupboards—breakfast cereal and milk and takeout containers. The medicine cabinet in the front bathroom was empty, and he pulled aside the cactus shower curtain to look at the bathtub, its surface so white and spotless that it might never have been used. In the master he heard the water go off. Truman went back in and sat in the easy chair in the corner.

Grant grinned at him as he came out of the bathroom, pulling open his underwear drawer and stepping into a pair.

"I feel like a stripper," Grant said.

"You're doing the opposite of that."

"But you're watching me the way guys watch strippers."

"Your body is better than any stripper ever," Truman said. "It's like looking at good art."

Grant guffawed at that as he buttoned his shirt, clearly flattered. "Let's get out of here, detective."

After he set the alarm, they went out to the driveway and climbed into the big car. It was absurdly roomy, with space for three or four people in the front seat alone. A chrome plaque affixed to the wood-grain dashboard read ELDORADO in tight script.

"So you think I could be a stripper," Grant said, his elbow on the back of the seat as he looked out the rear window and deftly swung into the street.

"You could work at any burly-cue in town," Truman said, gazing out the side window.

"What's a burly-cue?"

"It's an old word for a strip club."

"You mean 'burlesque'?" Grant demanded, glancing at him as he braked for the light at Sunset.

"I've heard it pronounced that way, but I'm pretty sure it's *burly-cue*."

"I'm pretty sure it's not," Grant said, and chuckled.

"This thing rides smooth," Truman said, "but even with the top up, it's pretty noisy inside."

"That's the price of having a convertible."

"I guess it would be nice in summer."

"I know you don't drive," Grant said, "but what about your friend Celeste?"

"Oh, yeah, she totally has a car."

"I know that," Grant said. "I didn't get a look at it when you came by the other night. What's her ride?"

"You mean the brand? It's smaller than this one, and not that old. I know it's blue."

He scoffed. "I hope you're better at finding people than you are at car stuff."

Truman watched the city roll by as they cruised down Sunset. The midday traffic was sluggish, and lots of people were out on the side-walk. The big red car drew a lot of looks, and double-takes, and once in a while someone would flash a thumbs-up. Maybe that was part of the reason Grant had chosen it: driving this thing demanded attention.

Once they were downtown, Grant pulled into a garage under one of the office towers on Fig.

"It's business hours," Truman said as they rolled down the ramp. "This is going to cost you a fortune."

"I can't really leave this car at a meter," he said, frowning.

That made sense, Truman thought. Even pulled in tight to the curb, it would probably block half the adjacent travel lane.

They rode the elevator together up to the lobby, and Truman paused when they got to the street.

"I had fun today," Grant said.

Truman put a hand on his bicep and leaned in to kiss him good-bye. Grant wasn't expecting it, and gave him a brief awkward cheek-peck and a pat on the shoulder before pulling away. Was he embarrassed to kiss a guy in public? Truman wondered, watching him head up the sidewalk. Maybe it was something else—like not wanting to be seen by whoever he was meeting.

Standing on the sidewalk in the shadow of the building, he watched Grant cross the street and turn onto Seventh, not once glancing over his shoulder, then disappearing from sight. Who was he going to meet? If he really were selling fancy

Westside real estate, he wouldn't be doing it here.

Truman hustled to follow him, stepping into the traffic in a break between cars and trotting to avoid an oncoming bus. Grant was tall, and Truman quickly caught sight of him. His shiny bald head stood out in the sea of pedestrians on the crowded sidewalk. Matching the pace of the people walking behind the guy, Truman was able to get closer without fear of being noticed.

A block farther along, Grant went inside the low rail fence of a sidewalk café. Truman stepped out of the stream of pedestrians, pausing close to the shop windows a few yards away. A guy in a bright blue dress shirt, beefy and dark and with a thick mustache, rose from a table at the end of the patio and greeted him. Truman couldn't hear what they were saying, and they didn't embrace, but the interaction was relaxed, like they knew each other well.

They sat down together. If only he could listen in. No way could Truman go into the patio and sit nearby, not without risking Grant noticing him. But they were sitting close to the next street corner, right at the patio fence at the end of the building. Maybe he could overhear them from there.

Turning back the way he'd come, he went up the side street, walking fast. Two more left turns and he was approaching the corner where Grant was sitting. He stopped when he caught sight of the railing for the café, and stood with his back against the concrete wall of the building, his heart pounding. People walked past, oblivious to Truman, but to make it look like he wasn't up to something, he pulled out his phone and gazed at the blank screen.

When he crept closer to the corner and leaned forward slightly, he could see the edge of a fleshy blue-clad shoulder—that was the guy sitting with Grant. Listening intently, he could hear them talking, but it was in Spanish. Was it someone else? But no, that was definitely Grant's voice. Truman never would have guessed that Grant spoke Spanish. Even when he'd asked Celeste about her name the other night, he hadn't revealed that about himself, hadn't copped to any worldliness or depth beyond the assumptions they'd made about him. Who was this guy?

More pressing right now was how he was going to understand their conversation. Maybe he could phone Celeste's dad to listen and translate for him. But that was a lot to explain. Then it struck him—he could record them and have someone translate it later. Why hadn't he thought of that sooner? Fumbling with his phone, he started the audio recorder, then held the device near the wall, as close to the corner as he could without looking suspicious.

A moment later a guy with a huge red beard

and a grubby military-green overcoat shuffled toward him, his shoes sharply slapping the pavement with each step. Glancing at the source of the noise, he saw that his sneakers didn't have laces in them, and flopped as he walked. Truman avoided eye contact as the guy approached, and instinctively stopped breathing through his nose. Living adjacent to Skid Row, he already knew all too well what homelessness smelled like. *Keep moving,* Truman thought, his eyes on the pavement, willing him not to stop. *Please don't bug me.* But that wasn't going to happen. Standing alone against a wall, he was too enticing a target.

"What are you doing?" the guy asked, stopping in front of Truman.

"Get out of here," Truman said under his breath, and gestured with his chin.

"You can't just hang around on street corners. That's called loitering."

Truman waved him away, vigorously flapping his arm.

"Give me a dollar," the guy said, staring at him.

Truman sighed and dug in his pants, then handed him a single. "Now leave," he hissed.

"Give me another dollar."

Around the corner on the café patio he heard the scrape of a metal chair shifting on concrete. Looking sideways and leaning ahead, he saw that Grant's companion was on his feet. Their meeting must be over. Ignoring the homeless guy, Truman turned on his heel and walked up the side street, breathing hard. A few steps later he remembered to turn off the audio recorder. He'd missed most of the conversation, but hopefully he'd captured something interesting.

The library was just a couple of blocks away, and Truman found a quiet bench under the trees in the little park out front, inhaling the fresh scent of the damp grass. The long shadows of the end of the day stretched across the lawn, darkening the nearby street.

Once he'd put his earbuds in, he listened to the recording he'd made. There was a lot of noise—cars, and other people talking, and then the homeless guy's flappy shoes—but both men's voices were audible. He sent Celeste a text:

Where you at?

Her reply came almost instantaneously:

At the gallery. On my way home in an hour.

Truman replied:

Can I swing by your place later?

He grinned when he got her one-syllable reply:

Sure.

It didn't give him enough time to go home first, and since he was already sitting in front of the library, he went inside and down into the history department. Even though the knowledge wouldn't generate any revenue, and it wasn't really connected to Jaime or Grant, he wanted to read about the neighborhood where he'd met Jamie, the Anglo veteran who'd mussed his hair. He spent a while locating the relevant books, and found out that the area was technically part of Boyle Heights. Poring over the pages, he got lost in the history.

Eventually he took a couple of the volumes and checked them out, stuffing them in his backpack and then making his way to the train. The cars were crowded with early evening commuters, but Celeste's stop wasn't far, and from there her family's ancient Victorian with its tiny yard was just a few minutes' walk.

Every house on the block had a fence fronting the sidewalk, and Ernesto took care of their place—the trees were tidy and groomed, and unlike some of the neighbors, the structure had all its shingles and a good paint job. Celeste pulled open the door when he knocked. She was dressed for a night in—sweatpants and a drab olive sweater.

"Where are your parents?" he asked, following her into the kitchen. "I wanted to talk to Ernesto."

"Still at work, probably," she said, pushing her hair back. "He'll be here soon. Want some tea? I just made it."

Truman pulled off his backpack and sat at the kitchen table while she poured two mugfuls from an earthen teapot.

"Why do you need my father?" she asked, sitting across from him.

Truman explained how he'd followed Grant, eavesdropped on him, and taped his conversation.

"How cool is that?" she said. "You just happened to run into him downtown?"

"I hitched a ride with him from his house."

"You went over there to get paid?"

"Not exactly."

Celeste sighed, setting down her mug. "No judgment, but if you keep sleeping with Grant, how can you be objective about any of this?"

"I can be objective," Truman said, frowning. "I'm working for the guy. It's not like I want to marry him."

She scoffed. "He's so hot that I bet you already picked out your wedding tux."

"Anyway, I was kind of surprised he could speak Spanish."

"That's exactly my point—the fact that you're surprised means you've already made a bunch of assumptions about him."

Truman threw up his hands. "I'm not all

crushed out and deluded here. I'm collecting more information. Why didn't his language skills come up when we were socializing? It seems so basic."

"It's definitely more evidence of his deception."

He sighed and sipped his tea.

"I went on an excursion today myself," Celeste said, and told him about meeting Bibi.

"I love that you thought of asking her," Truman said. "If you get invited back for a pool party, I want to go."

"I suspect Bibi's pool parties are women-only," she said.

The front door swung open, and Celeste's mother stepped in from the darkness, dressed in a charcoal-gray pantsuit, her black hair pulled back. Pinned on her lapel was a gold name tag embossed with a corporate logo and MARÍA. Truman rose to greet her, exchanging a kiss on the cheek.

"You look good," she said, giving him the once-over. "You must be working more."

"I guess I've been busy," he said.

"Stay and eat with us," she said, and stepped toward the back of the house. "It'll be later, though. I need to change and get to a meeting."

Once María had gone, Celeste said, "You could ask her to translate."

"It sounds like she's in a rush. Plus I worry

that it might be something unsavory."

She frowned. "My mother's not exactly a shrinking violet. But I guess my father knows you better."

"He knows me intimately," Truman said. "He rewired my entire loft, and put walls around the bathroom."

"Among other favors."

"I wonder if he helps me because he thinks I might magically turn straight one day and marry you."

She chuckled. "He's under no such delusion. He likes you. He doesn't have any sons of his own. Besides, I think he'd want a better earner as a son-in-law."

The door opened again and Ernesto stepped inside. Barrel-chested and with graying hair, his belly protruded a little over his belt.

"Truman," he boomed. "Great to see you. Are you keeping out of trouble?"

"Mostly," he said, and rose to greet him.

María stepped in from the back of the house, out of her work garb now, with her hair down and wearing jeans.

"I'm running late," she said, and kissed Ernesto before she went out the front door.

"Where's she going in such a hurry?" Celeste demanded.

"A cake fight," Ernesto said, and dropped his

keys on the kitchen counter.

"You know," Celeste said, "when you talk like a misogynist, it just makes you seem older."

"*¡Ay!*" Ernesto yelped, and grabbed his chest in mock distress. "You're breaking my heart."

"What's a cake fight?" Truman asked.

"It's her women's group," Celeste said. "Apparently they have coffee and cake as their snack."

"And they fight over it?"

Ernesto threw his head back in a deep hearty laugh.

"That's just my father's sexist assumptions about how women resolve disagreements."

"Always so serious," Ernesto said to her, and to Truman, "You have no idea what it's like to be the only man in a house full of women."

"There's only two women," Celeste said.

He raised his eyebrows and met her gaze. "That's a lot."

"Truman wants you to translate something," she said, waving her hand to change the subject.

"I taped a conversation," Truman said, pulling out his phone.

"Let me change my shirt first," Ernesto said, and went into the back of the house. "If my daughter had learned Spanish properly," he called to them, "She could translate it for you."

"Like that's my fault," she shot back.

When Ernesto returned, he was wearing a

roomy sweatshirt, and pulled out a chair to join them. Truman set his phone in the middle of the table and played the recording. Cocking his head, Ernesto squinted as he listened. After a while he reached out to tap the screen and pause the playback.

"I can only pick out a few things over the traffic noise," he said, "but I think they're talking about driving in Sonora, or driving to Sonora."

"That's at Tucson, right? The Sonoran Desert?"

"It's part of Mexico. I think that's what they're talking about."

"So they're taking a road trip to Mexico?"

"I'm not sure it's about them," Ernesto said, and tapped on the screen to resume the playback.

On the recording, a much louder voice demanded, "What are you doing?"

Ernesto recoiled at the sudden volume. "Who's that?"

"Some homeless guy," Truman said.

They listened to the rest of the clip, but the voices of Grant and his companion weren't audible over Truman's own conversation.

Ernesto chuckled. "'Give me another dollar.' That guy had you on the hook."

"I guess I'm on his sucker list now."

Picking up the phone, he said, "Let me hear it again." Holding it closer to his ear, he listened through the recording once more. "That's really all I can get—someone is going to be driving in Sonora."

"Thanks anyway," Truman said.

Celeste pulled out her phone, which was buzzing, and checked the screen.

"It's him," she said intently, looking up at Truman.

"Him who?" Ernesto demanded, folding his arms.

Celeste ignored him, staring at the phone and letting it ring a little longer before she picked up.

"This is Penelope."

Ernesto scowled at her and then got up. As he walked out, he caught Truman's gaze and grinned, shaking his head.

"Hey, pretty lady," Jaime said. "I'm glad you answered. I want to see you again."

"I'm up for that," Celeste said.

"Do you want to come over? I'm in Westlake. Not far from where we met."

"You live around there?"

"I'm crashing at a friend's—he's away for a while. His place is near the hospital. Do you know it?"

"We should meet out somewhere," she said quickly. "Not the Stallion—your ex might be there."

"How about the beach?"

"I'm not really a beach person."

"I meant we could go for a walk on the pier. I don't want to go suntan in the middle of winter, and get sand all up in my shorts."

"I guess that works," she said, and chuckled. Before she ended the call, they made a plan to meet.

"Right on," Truman said emphatically. "You did it."

He held up a palm, and Celeste reached up to slap it, a celebratory high-five.

"I'm meeting him tomorrow."

"I heard—the pier. That's very romantic. Are you blushing right now?"

"Shut up," she said firmly.

"I'm so glad he called."

"I guess all that flirting worked."

"We're getting close," Truman said. "I can feel it."

"The pier is a busy public place," she said. "You could even get Grant to meet us there, and end it that way."

"You mean ambush Jaime?" he said, incredulous. "I was thinking I'd just tell Grant where to find him once I knew."

She sipped her tea, thoughtful for a moment. "That's probably smart—that way neither one of us would be in the middle of it."

"Can you ask Jaime where he's staying?"

"He just told me he was at some friend's in

Westlake. I'm sure I'll be able to get specifics tomorrow."

"I wonder if I should crash your date, and talk to Jaime myself," Truman said. "I could ask him why he's avoiding Grant."

Celeste frowned. "Why would you do that? You're getting paid to locate the guy, not to make sure everyone's comfortable with the situation. Confronting him like that might spook him. Jaime could disappear, and you'll never get paid."

"Still, don't you want to know why Grant's lying about everything?"

"Your loyalty should be to the guy who's paying you."

"Even if he's a lowlife?"

"Especially if he's a lowlife."

Truman sighed. "I know you're right."

"And you're not coming on my date. Let's see what I can learn tomorrow, and we'll go from there."

"Fine," he said. "No ambushes."

———◆———

Riding the train back toward his own neighborhood, Truman thought things through. Celeste was probably right that he wasn't being objective about Grant. His perfect body, perfect skin, that heart-melting smile. Surprising Jaime in public was a bad idea, but she was right that Truman couldn't drag this out indefinitely, couldn't ask Grant to keep paying him while he decided how to get them together. But Jaime had called—and Truman was getting close to answering his client's ask. Watching the concrete tunnel flash by, he grinned at the success.

NINE

In the morning, getting ready for work, Celeste prepared for her outing with Jaime. It was happening later in the day, but she had to dress for it now. Flats and black Capri pants, she decided. They weren't especially flattering, but jeans were wrong for the beach, and so was a skirt, with all that wind.

Opening her jewelry box, she lifted out the tray and found the little prescription bottle of Ritalin. There weren't many left—she'd need to get these replenished. That took a bit of work, wrangling with medical people, but it was doable. She wasn't an addict, she knew, because addicts had no self-control. Celeste was in control of how she used this stuff, taking it only when it was safe and appropriate. Stuffing a tablet in her pants pocket, she fixed her hair in the bathroom mirror, then drove to work.

The gallery was dark when she got in, pausing to turn off the alarm before she flipped on the lights and unlocked the front door, twisting the little sign in the window to read OPEN. Saffron wasn't here yet; she was coming in after lunch so that Celeste could take the afternoon to meet Jaime.

Celeste was absorbed in her computer screen, reading an article online about sales trends in the art industry, when the front door opened and a woman stepped in. She didn't recognize her at first, wearing a ball cap and big sunglasses, jeans and a bomber jacket. Rich people in Los Angeles dressed like homeless people half the time, and she worked to assess whether this visitor was more likely to drop fifty grand on a painting or start raving about Jesus and pee on a wall. Sometimes the only determinant was olfactory. But Celeste wasn't going to have to eighty-six this person. The spiky blond hair around her ears, that wry smile, the swagger—it was Bibi, the classic car dealer.

"This place sure is quiet," Bibi said, pulling off her glasses.

"It picks up on the weekend," Celeste lied. "Unfortunately Saffron isn't in yet. Did you have a meeting?"

"I'm here to see you, girl," Bibi said, stepping closer to her desk.

Celeste's eyebrows shot up. "I guess I should be flattered. I'm sure you're a busy woman."

"Are you going to ask me to sit down?"

"Of course," Celeste said, and waved to the chair in front of her desk. "Can I get you a drink? I think there's soda water, and maybe some gin."

"No booze," Bibi said, looking around and languorously stretching her arms, arching her back. "A soda water would be nice."

Celeste rose and went to the storeroom under the stairs, stooping to look in the fridge. Bibi wouldn't care that it wasn't in a glass, she decided, and went back with two little bottles, handing one to her guest before she sat in her desk chair.

Bibi cracked the cap open with a hiss, leaning back in her chair and spreading her knees apart as she took a pull on the bottle.

Celeste smiled politely, hands folded on the desktop, watching her and waiting for her to speak.

"So I looked into that '72 Road Runner you were asking about," Bibi said finally. "I think I might have found the pink slip."

"What's the pink slip?" Celeste said.

"It means the title," Bibi said, gesturing with her bottle. "The paperwork on who owns the car. If it's the right vehicle, it belongs to a woman named Vanessa Martínez."

"That sounds right," Celeste said, leaning forward. "How did you figure it out?"

"It's not really protected information. I called in a favor. You said it belonged to a guy, but maybe Vanessa is his mama, or his girlfriend. Does he have the same name?"

"He doesn't," Celeste said. That was a lie—it was indeed Jaime's surname—but there was no reason Bibi needed to know all the details. "Although that doesn't mean it's the wrong car. Was there an address?"

"That's the only other piece of information I got." She pulled a sheet of paper out of her hip pocket and handed it across the desk.

Folding it open, Celeste found the name and an address written in blue ballpoint. Deciphering the looping handwriting, her pulse quickened. She didn't recognize the street name, but the zip code was the same as the one for her own home.

"I don't know how to thank you for this," Celeste said, looking up at her.

"I have some ideas about that."

"Would it involve hanging out at your pool?"

Bibi laughed. "We can definitely talk about that too. I was thinking you could do some work for me. Saffron says you know your stuff."

"In the art world? Sure."

"I commissioned some pieces through her before. Modern art with cars in it. I can't afford to do that again, but maybe you could keep an eye out for paintings in that genre. Pitch them to me, and if I want them, I'll make sure you get a commission."

"I'd love to track down art for you," Celeste said. "It's not even work for me."

"Good." Bibi nodded and reached into her pants pocket again, producing a business card and setting it on the table. "That's me. Call anytime."

Celeste picked up the card, embossed in black lettering over stylized red flames:

BIBI CARLBERG
BEAUTIFUL CARS

"You might want to mention it to Saffron too," Bibi said. "I don't want to go behind her back."

"That's probably wise. She might want a cut for the gallery."

She waved dismissively. "I'm sure we can work something out." Sipping from her bottle, she met Celeste's gaze. "So why are you looking for this particular car? I can't believe it's just about stalking a guy."

"I'm trying to figure out his background. Specifically where he lives."

Her eyes narrowed. "How well do you know him? Can't you just ask him?"

Celeste laughed. "I'm seeing him later today. Maybe I'll do that."

Bibi lingered a little longer, chatty but less flirty than she'd been yesterday, before rising and pulling her sunglasses back on. After she left, Celeste realized she should have walked her out to her car to see what she was driving. Undoubtedly it was flashy, and as her flaming business card proclaimed, it was sure to be something beautiful.

Most likely Bibi had followed up on researching Jaime's car because she'd taken a personal interest in Celeste, she decided. But she could handle a little flirting, and even though she'd never let it go anywhere, or start hanging out around Bibi's pool, it was an ego boost that someone found her desirable. More important, she might make some money. Celeste had to grin. Bibi was such a wheeler-dealer. "Modern art with cars in it" wasn't actually a genre, or even a thing, and it was far from the highbrow pieces most wealthy collectors wanted, but if Bibi had a budget for art, Celeste could make it work.

Picking up her phone, she dialed Truman.

When he answered, she said, "Sometimes being hot is a way to get ahead."

"Please tell me you didn't sleep with Saffron," Truman said.

"Ew! Why would you say that?" she demanded. "That car dealer, Bibi, came by the gallery this morning."

"I remember you said she was flirty. She

definitely thinks you're hot."

"Technically, I am hot, and she simply picked up on that objective and immutable fact," Celeste said. "Anyway, she found an address that might be connected to Jaime." She told him about Bibi's visit, and the name on the vehicle title.

"It has to be the car," Truman said. "How many people named Martínez would own the exact same antique?"

"The address is in my neighborhood too," Celeste said. "I'll text it to you."

"I'm totally going to check it out today. You're amazing," Truman said. "You should be the detective."

She laughed. "I just asked the woman some questions."

"But you found exactly the right person to ask."

After she ended the call, Celeste took a photo of the paper Bibi had given her and texted it to Truman. His enthusiasm put a smile on her face, and the gallery didn't seem as dank and empty for a while. After lunch, when Saffron showed up, Celeste tidied up her desk and headed toward the metro. Waiting on the platform, she fished the Ritalin tablet out of her pocket and crunched it between her teeth.

———•———

Truman was lounging in bed when he talked to Celeste, well into his second coffee but still not dressed. Looking at the photo she'd sent him of the handwritten note, he checked the address on a map. As she'd said, it was in Celeste's neighborhood, a house on a block crowded with tiny century-old bungalows. Simpler than the ones on Celeste's street, these had no Victorian flourishes—in this view they were just cramped and basic proto–tract houses.

The only way he was going to figure out if Jaime lived there was to go, he decided. Draining his mug, he got dressed and slung on his backpack, then headed down to the street.

Thoroughly warmed up from the walk by the time he got to the metro, he changed trains downtown and rode to Boyle Heights. Vanessa's house wasn't far from the station. Walking up on it, he shoved his hands in his jacket pockets and slowed his pace, taking it in.

The front yard had a heavy fence around it, like every other house on the block, and a sprawling ficus tree obscured part of the structure. Bougainvillea grew along the driveway, pruned to hug the fence bordering the next property, a riot of fuchsia despite the fact that it was the middle of winter. The curtains were drawn, he could tell, behind the bars on the windows, painted black to blend in. The entrance was less subtle in terms of security, with a heavy steel mesh door facing the yard.

At the end of the driveway was a little one-car garage. It had the same shallow hipped roof and the same shingles as the house, making it the same vintage, based on the old-school side-mounted doors, built when cars weren't very wide. But it was definitely wide enough to fit a '72 Road Runner.

Truman stopped at the gate across the driveway. Far more modern than the structures, it was mounted on a rail and had a motor that would retract it into a slot behind the adjoining fence, probably by remote control. The fence and the gate were low enough that he could almost step over. But then he'd basically be a prowler. A car drove up the street, and Truman glanced at it. The driver ignored him. No one was out in their yards at this time of day either. He really wanted to look in that garage; it could provide the key piece of information he needed. But this gate was here for a reason.

Biff Sturgis talked a lot about stakeouts, and he'd probably advise setting up operatives to monitor the place around the clock. But Truman didn't have operatives, and who had time to sit around for hours on end like that? In the chapter about dealing with the law, Biff said, "The only rule you need to guide your actions is what you can reasonably get away with." That definitely fit the present circumstances. The only question was, could Truman get away with it?

With a last look around the street to make sure he wasn't being observed, Truman took a deep breath and grabbed the top rail of the gate. Heaving one leg over, he cleared it easily, hopping on one foot, then swung his other leg. His backpack shifted as he moved, throwing him off balance, and he tumbled to his butt in the driveway.

Idiot, he admonished himself. The one thing a prowler didn't need was to draw attention, and this kind of slapstick definitely would. Massaging the hand that had connected with the concrete and quickly checking it for damage, he swatted the dust off his pants and walked up the driveway toward the garage.

The big doors had a decent coat of paint, which was unusual considering their age and the fact that lots of buildings in the neighborhood suffered neglect. What he hadn't seen from the street was a padlock, dangling over a hasp. Grabbing it and giving it a twist to check, he found it was firmly locked.

"Damn it," he muttered, stepping back. But maybe there was another way. Along the top of the doors were square little windows, a dozen panes in a row, just a few inches above his head.

He didn't need to get inside—all he needed to do was have a look.

Setting his backpack on the concrete, he crouched in front of one of the doors and jumped as high as he could, trying to see in. The pane was dusty, and he reached up to wipe it before he tried again. In the brief instant that his view was level with the window, he could see it was dark inside, and there were boxes piled at the back, but no vehicle. One more time, he decided, to make sure, and he leapt up, peering inside.

"Looking for something?" a woman's voice called to him, just as his feet reconnected with the ground.

Whirling toward the house, he saw who'd spoken to him, standing outside the front door, which was hanging open now. In her fifties, maybe, with dark hair styled and slicked back, she was dressed to be outside, in a dark-blue pea coat and high-cuffed black trousers. Below them she wore stiletto-heeled pumps. This was no relative of Jaime's—she was too Anglo, too affluent, that makeup job too Westside. In this heavily Latin neighborhood, she looked completely out of place. Hands on her hips, she stood watching him, but she didn't look especially concerned.

"I thought there might be a car in there," Truman said, scooping up his backpack, ready to bolt down the driveway.

"Were you trying to steal it?"

He scowled and pulled on his bag. "I'm not a thief. The title says it's registered to this address."

"So you're a repo guy," she said, raising her eyebrows. "I get it. She owes me money too."

Truman sighed with relief and stepped toward the house. At least this woman wasn't going to call the cops on him.

"Do you live here?" he asked.

She scoffed. "I live in Pasadena."

"So you're a debt collector?"

"I own it," she said flatly. "I'm not surprised the car's not here. It was a chocolate-brown number, right? One of those peppy little Fiats?"

"Something like that. Is she home?"

The woman smiled and pushed her hair behind her ear. "I'm afraid my good fortune is your bad luck. I evicted her a couple of weeks ago. The sheriff came and everything."

"What was the family name?"

"Bingels," she said. "Is that who leased the Fiat?"

"It was under a different name," Truman said.

"Christ, how many of them were living here? It's a small house."

"Was there a Martínez on the lease?"

"The only tenant I knew about was named Hilda Bingels."

"How long did she live here?"

"Three years," she said. "Are you sure you have the right address?"

"This is the place," Truman said, although he wasn't at all sure of that now. The note that the car dealer had given Celeste was written by hand; maybe Bibi had screwed something up when she transcribed it.

The woman eyed him for a minute, then waggled the keys she was holding. "She left some stuff, if you want to look around."

"That might be helpful," Truman said, and stepped toward the house.

"I'm Maxine, by the way."

"David," Truman said, and followed her inside.

It wasn't just some stuff, he saw—it was everything. The front room still looked occupied, with a full set of living room furniture, a pile of magazines on the coffee table, jackets hanging inside the front door. Truman stepped into the kitchen, where there was a box of soda crackers sitting open on the counter, and dishes in the sink.

"Are you sure they've moved out?" Truman asked, looking around.

"What did you say?" Maxine called from down the hall.

Truman followed her voice into one of the bedrooms, where there were clothes strewn on the floor, the bed unmade.

"Someone's still living here," Truman said.

"There's a pot of oatmeal on the stove. It's cold, but still."

"I'm pretty sure she's gone," Maxine said, shooting him a nonchalant smile and stepping around the end of the bed.

Truman studied her, furrowing his brow. Either she was delusional, or something else was going on, and he just wasn't getting it.

"Doesn't this look comfortable?" she said, nodding to the bed and winking at him.

"Are you kidding me right now?" Truman demanded.

"That depends. Do you think I'm kidding you?"

"I only date guys," Truman said, raising his voice. "And even if you were a guy, I wouldn't get busy with you on someone else's bed. Look at this place, Maxine—there's mail on the dresser, and I'm standing on a pair of skanky underpants. Someone's living here."

"I guess it's true what they say," she said. "All the good ones are gay."

"I'm not a good one," Truman said intently. "Trust me."

"You don't seem all that hard-boiled," she said, frowning. "I know you sneak around and take people's cars in the night, but not *my* car. Do you carry a sidearm?"

Truman sighed impatiently. "I think we're

losing sight of the bigger picture. Are you sure your tenant moved out? Did the sheriff tell you to change the locks? Maybe someone's squatting in here."

"You know, you might be good for my son," she said, still eyeing him and cocking her head. "He may be a little young for you, but he's a sweetheart. He's not out yet. I keep waiting. Maybe you could help him step out of his shell. Be the warmth that unfurls the rosebud's petals."

"Maxine, focus," Truman demanded. "I'm not going to date your son. What the hell is going on here?"

"My tenant left a mess, is what happened," she said, and then raised a finger. "Hold on. Did you hear that?"

"Hear what?"

"The gate. We should go." She pushed past him and went into the hallway, her pace decisive.

Truman followed and saw her ducking out the front door. When he got there, stepping outside, the gate to the street had rolled open, and a dark-red pickup sat in the driveway. It was scuffed and battered, and in the bed was a utility frame with a stepladder lashed to it. A guy climbed out of the driver's side, glaring at Maxine. Thickset and swarthy, wearing jeans and a gray hoodie with the hood down, he looked blue-collar, which fit the truck, and fit the house, and fit the neighborhood a lot more than Pasadena Maxine.

"What the hell are you doing in my house?" he demanded, waving an arm at them.

"Hey, there," Maxine called to him, waggling her fingers in an offhand greeting. Leaning toward Truman, under her breath, she said, "You should run, Dave."

"What?" Truman said, feeling his heart start to pound.

"Run, sweetheart. That's what I'm going to do."

The new arrival slammed the door to his truck and started toward them, fists balled, his face contorted with anger. Not waiting for further encouragement, Truman bolted across the lawn, under the ficus, and vaulted over the fence, this time not losing his balance as his feet hit the sidewalk.

"Hey," the man shouted behind him, but Truman didn't slow down to look back. The guy looked like he could hold his own in a brawl, but he was carrying a few extra pounds, and Truman was pretty sure he could outrun him.

Sprinting until he reached the end of the block, he stopped to look back and saw Maxine, loping like a gazelle in her high heels, clopping audibly on the asphalt as she hustled across the street. Competent in the stilettos, she was moving fast. The guy came out of the driveway, his face red. His gaze followed Maxine as she turned onto the side street, and then he looked at Truman. Their eyes met for a moment, and Truman realized he'd paused for too long. The guy started running toward him, elbows pumping.

Truman bolted onto the side street, opposite the direction Maxine had gone, and ran as fast as he could, not slowing down at intersections, swiveling his head to scan for oncoming cars. When he reached the boulevard, with the metro station right across the street, he looked behind him. The guy was tenacious, half a block behind but still chasing him.

Darting into the street in a gap in the traffic, Truman zigzagged behind a bus to get to the other side. Descending into the metro was a risk—apart from the trains, there was only one way out. But there were cameras everywhere, and tons of witnesses, so at least the guy might be dissuaded from clocking him. And there was a train—he could hear it, the rumble growing as it approached the station.

He hustled down the stairs two at a time, feeling the breeze in his face from the air pushed out of the tunnel by the oncoming mass. Just as the train came to a stop, he reached the platform. The doors opened, and Truman dived into a car and sat down, trying to be inconspicuous, avoiding the gaze of a passenger sitting opposite, curious as to why he was flushed and panting. His chest heaved from fear and the exertion of his run.

"Come on," he muttered, willing the doors to close, watching the stairs outside them at the end of the platform. Just as the doors finally rumbled closed, his pursuer appeared, scuffed work boots trotting down the steps. The train started to move, and Truman heaved a sigh of relief, working to catch his breath. That had been close. The guy stood on the platform and peered into the train as it rolled by, panting as hard as Truman was.

"You'd better run," he shouted, even though he didn't have his eyes on Truman, his words muffled through the glass. "I fought for this country."

What did that have to do with anything, Truman wondered, and then lost sight of him as the train accelerated into the tunnel. What the hell had just happened?

TEN

Not long after she left the gallery, Celeste was climbing the escalator out of the ground at Seventh Street. Jaime had agreed to meet her here—no way was she going to give him her home address or have him pick her up at her workplace. Going on a date with an actual straight guy was exciting, but she was under no illusion that Jaime was anything more than a rake.

Celeste pulled on her dark sunglasses and waited near the agreed-on corner, her arms folded, watching the busy rush of office workers out running errands, checking out their haircuts and workaday outfits. The Ritalin made it all a little more interesting, made the colors pop.

"Penelope," a voice called. "Hey, Penelope."

It took her a moment to remember that meant her. Looking around, she spotted Jaime walking up, a quizzical grin on his face. He was wearing loose jeans and a white shirt, unbuttoned halfway down his chest.

"I thought I heard my name," she said.

"I thought maybe you were hard of hearing," he said, and then smiled. "You look great."

"Where's your car?"

"I'm in the red zone around the corner. Come on," he said, and for the briefest moment gently put his hand on the small of her back.

Celeste got a whiff of his cologne as they walked, and she looked him over, glancing sidelong, watching his confident stride. The guy had swagger. It didn't always work, that look, but with the right guy, swagger was hot.

As they came to the corner she spotted Jaime's car, matte black and with those sleek retro curves. He'd parked at a fire hydrant and left the flashers on. So this was the infamous Road Runner. Jaime stepped up to it and pulled open the passenger door, waiting while she climbed in.

When he went around and got behind the wheel, he pulled on a pair of mirrored sunglasses that were hanging from the visor. That was thoughtful, taking those off when he came to greet her. A lesser man wouldn't have risked a parking ticket either, would have just pulled up to the curb and honked at her. She eyed him as he shifted into gear and nosed into the traffic. *Work,* she reminded herself. This wasn't a real date. This was work.

"Sweet ride," she said. "How old is it?"

"It's a '72."

The experience was different than in a modern car, she realized, with the powerful old engine audible and rumbling at her feet. Jaime got moving fast but drove calmly, deftly manipulating the manual gearshift, navigating to the 10 for the ride out to the beach.

"So what does Penelope do for a living?" he asked, glancing over at her.

"I kind of manage an art gallery."

"Kind of?"

"The 'manage' part is unofficial. It's high-end, so there aren't a lot of buyers."

"So there's not a lot to manage. Do you get paid well?"

"I guess so, but overall it seems like a waste of an art history degree."

Jaime grinned at that, keeping his eyes on the stop-and-go traffic.

"What do you do?"

"I'm basically a courier," Jaime said. "I have some friends who are in the shipping business, and I work freelance for them."

"Driving a truck?"

He laughed. "More like logistics. Making sure shipments meet their deadlines."

"And you don't have to work on Wednesday afternoons?"

"There's a lot of down time."

When they got to the pier, Jaime shelled out for the good parking right next to it, rather than driving around looking for a cheaper option, like Celeste would have done if she were driving.

Rolling down his window, he handed the parking attendant a twenty and greeted him in Spanish. Celeste recognized the phrase he used, even though it was slang. Literally it was something like *Are you earning,* but it meant *How's business?* Watching Jaime cheerfully interact with the guy as he took his change, she wished he wasn't so pleasant, or such a good conversationalist, or so confident and calm. If only there was something to dislike, some red flag, the slightest turnoff—compartmentalizing this would be so much easier.

The pier wasn't crowded, probably because of the cool winter breeze off the water. They strolled leisurely on the wooden walkway, stopping in to see the antique carousel, then farther along pausing to watch a street performer who'd spray-painted himself silver. Jaime flipped a coin into his hat before they moved on.

At the end they leaned on the rail, with a view

of the vast Pacific, a couple of cargo ships and a lone sailboat on the horizon.

"Next stop, Manila," Jaime said.

"It's hard to fit in your mind how vast it is."

Celeste watched the waves for a while, and Jaime seemed content to stand with her in comfortable silence. Around them several people had lines in the water.

"I wonder what they're fishing for?" Celeste said.

"Whatever it is, I wouldn't eat it. Have you ever seen what goes into the storm sewers? In my neighborhood it's stuff you wouldn't want to have any contact with, never mind chowing down on it."

"You mean Westlake?"

"I grew up in Boyle Heights."

"Oh, yeah? What part?"

"My mom lives just up from the plaza. Where are your people from?"

"Whittier," Celeste said. It was an evasive lie, and before he could ask a follow-up question, she stood erect and pulled out her phone. "Selfie time."

Jaime dutifully turned his back to the sea and stood close, stretching his arm around her waist.

Celeste pulled off her sunglasses and said, "You too. Glasses off."

Jaime obliged and grinned sweetly, leaning into her from the hip as she held up her phone.

Once she'd snapped the photo, she showed it to him.

"You look great," he said. "Text that to me."

Looking at her phone again, Celeste sent it in a text to Truman. She wasn't about to send Jaime a photo of herself.

"Do you want to eat?" Jaime said finally.

"There's nothing decent here."

"So let's go up top."

Strolling on the pedestrian mall a few blocks away, they settled on a pizza place that had a patio, made cozy in the winter air by strategically placed heat lamps. While they were waiting for their food, Celeste pulled off her jacket and draped it over the back of her chair.

"So what's good art?" Jaime asked, frowning thoughtfully.

"You mean how do we choose artists for the gallery?"

"Not specifically. I mean, how can you tell if a painting is any good?"

She smiled. It was a way for him to connect with her, asking about something she was interested in, but he didn't have the same framework to talk about it.

"'Good' is totally subjective," she said. "It's like mushrooms on the pizza—good for me, not good for you. The way a lot of art is evaluated is just in terms of scarcity and demand. An artist's work is expensive if a lot of people want a piece of it. And if the artist is dead, there won't be any new ones created."

"So it's just like gasoline, or gold bricks?"

"Gasoline is fungible," Celeste said. "Artworks aren't."

"What does that mean, 'fungible'?" he said, frowning.

"It doesn't matter which gallon of gas you put in your car. They're all the same. Cash is like that—all twenty-dollar bills are interchangeable. Artworks are more like Marilyn's hoochie dress."

Jaime laughed. "You'll have to explain that too."

Celeste touched her fork, absently flipping it over as she spoke. "Someone bought Marilyn's hoochie dress recently for umpteen million dollars because she wore it in a movie. It's a unique piece because it was made for her. But if I made a hoochie dress, no one would pay that kind of money for it, even though it's also unique in the world. Artworks are like that. They're each unique. But there's no inherent value in an artwork except what you see in it."

"So how does one artist become more important than the rest?"

"Sometimes it's because they create a new style, or have a special technique, but often it's just like Marilyn—lots of people like her work, so it gets more attention, more demand. The art world is more about the analysis of critics and taste-makers, and the movies are more about popular appeal, but it's the same effect."

"I'd love to see you in a hoochie dress," Jaime said, holding her gaze.

"Play your cards right, and it might just happen," she said, and laughed. "So do you go on a lot of dates?"

Jaime folded his arms, a wry grin on his face. "Not with girls like you. You're a class act."

"Stop it," Celeste said firmly.

"It's not just flattery. I never meet girls like you. What were you doing in that crummy bar?"

"It's a long story," she said, relieved that the waiter chose that moment to present their pizza.

"I admit I don't have the best track record," Jaime said, sliding a slice off the tray.

"Married and divorced?" Celeste said, eyeing him.

"I have enough trouble being single. Norma, the girl I was meeting that night—she's totally ghosted me. Won't even take my calls."

"You slept with someone else," she said. "You told me that yourself."

Jaime looked down at his plate, setting his slice on it. "I do stupid things sometimes. No excuses."

Watching him, Celeste sighed. It took an

honest man to admit something like that. Why wasn't he more of a dick, more of a liar?

———•———

After they'd eaten, back on the pedestrian mall, Jaime casually put his arm around her shoulder. "Should we head east?"

"It's been nice," she said, and looped her arm around his waist.

When they climbed into the Road Runner, Jaime started the engine to get the air moving, then leaned toward her. "Want to come to my place?"

"I can't," she said gently.

"I understand." Looking at her chin, his eyes went soft, and he leaned toward her.

She met his mouth, firm and warm and scratchy with stubble around the sides, and got lost in it. Jaime ran his hand into her hair, gently pulling her closer. She put her palm on the side of his neck. She could feel his pulse. Jaime's fingers gently settled on her knee, then his very warm palm. He slid his hand to the inside of her thigh, moving slowly, making her heart pound. Eventually she pulled back.

"Time to drive?" he said.

"I'm afraid so."

Jaime sighed and absently adjusted his crotch.

As he navigated toward the freeway, Celeste said, "Why are you staying at a friend's place?"

"With my job I move around a lot. I'm in Orange County, San Diego, San Berdoo. I used to stay with my mom sometimes, but these days I do lots of couch surfing."

"You said your friend's place was by the hospital? Is it an apartment, or a whole house?"

"It's a ratty little apartment," he said, and grinned at her, reaching over to lace his fingers into hers.

She couldn't press him any more about where he lived, not without it sounding suspicious. If she went there with him, she'd quickly find out the address, but no way was she doing that.

Traffic wasn't bad on the 10, and as they approached the split to the 110, Jaime asked, "Do you want me to take you to Whittier?"

"I have to be downtown," she said. "But it's sweet of you to offer."

A few minutes later Jaime pulled up to the same corner where they'd met, a block from the metro. As she climbed out, she thanked him for driving.

"You know I'm going to call you," he said, holding her gaze for a moment, and then pulled away.

Standing back from the corner, Celeste sighed and pulled out her phone. She hated how nice he was, and hated that she'd made zero progress. She'd had one thing to find out about the guy—where he lived—and after spending half the damn day with him, she hadn't managed to figure it out. She texted Truman:

> Jaime just dropped me downtown. Want to meet to debrief?

<hr>

Back home and lounging on his sofa, Truman had been going over the encounter with Maxine and the man in the hoodie who'd pulled up in the truck. Was she really his landlord? The guy had been angry enough to chase him several blocks, and he was a big dude—if he'd caught up to him, Truman might have suffered a beat-down, or at the very least would have had to explain himself to the cops. Nothing Maxine had told him connected the house to Jaime or Vanessa Martínez, whoever she was. The guy who'd chased him into the metro might have been a Martínez, but there was no way to figure that out now. Maxine had been odd, and inappropriate, and glib, and Truman had the sinking feeling that he actually might have helped her break into someone's house.

When Celeste sent the photo of her and Jaime, he studied it closely. Jaime was grinning at the camera, his hair ruffled by the breeze. Truman had to admit he was pretty good-looking. No way was this guy related to Maxine, based on his coloring, but he could be a relative of the guy who drove up in the red truck. Jaime knew how to smile for a photo, knew how to maximize his assets. It probably enabled his sleazy behavior, that sweet disarming expression. Celeste was grinning too. Truman zoomed in on the image, studying her face. She definitely looked too happy.

Reading her newer text, he wrote back:

I'll be at that coffee place in 20.

Pulling on his jacket, he headed for the metro, and was soon walking into the coffee-house. Celeste was at a table near the window, cradling a coffee cup. Sliding into the opposite chair, Truman gave her the once-over.

"Cute outfit," he said. "You look exhausted— did you sleep with him?"

Celeste scoffed. "Not everyone is as slutty as you. Although we did make out a little in his car before we came back."

"Seriously? You didn't have to do that."

"I didn't do it as research. I was surprised how ordinary he is, how real. Based on what Norma said, I expected him to be a swaggering liar."

"Just because he's personable doesn't mean he's not a player."

"I know that. But I kind of enjoyed hanging out with him."

"You can't get a crush on this guy," Truman

said. "He already admitted to you that he's a serial cheater, and he's my target."

"I'm not crushing on him," she said, frowning. "I'm investigating your target."

"You thought I was all blinded by foxy Grant. Maybe you're blinded by Jaime."

"Truman, chill," she insisted. "I was just having fun with it. I know he's a heel, and I know how to keep some distance."

"Let me get a coffee," he said, and went up to the counter.

When he returned, Celeste had steeled herself for the part that was hardest to tell. "I didn't manage to find out where he lives. I asked him, but he just said he couch-surfs a lot."

"So there might not even be a place to tell Grant about. That's not optimal." Truman sighed and sipped at his espresso. "But at least we know that now."

"What did you find at the address Bibi gave me?"

"It was extremely weird," he said, and told her about what had happened, how he and Maxine both ran away, how the guy had chased him into the metro.

Celeste shook her head in disbelief. "You're lucky you got away. And she was running in heels? She's definitely a crazy person. The whole thing is crazy."

"True, but she had a key to get in there. I think maybe she really was the landlord. I couldn't tell if the guy in the hoodie recognized her or not."

"Do you think he actually lived there?"

"He had some way to open the gate," Truman said, "and he was extremely pissed to see us coming out of the house."

"But you still don't know if the place has any connection to Jaime."

"Maxine said the tenant's name was Bingels."

Celeste scoffed. "She also told you no one was living there."

"I guess it's a dead end."

"Maybe not all of it. Jaime told me today that he grew up in my neighborhood. Even if that was the wrong house, there's a good chance my parents will know his family. I can get my mom to ask around."

"Great idea," Truman said. Finally some good news. "So did Jaime say where he works?"

"He was extremely cagey about that. It made me think he's doing something that's not legit. Logistics for a friend's shipping business, he said."

"Grant said that too—he was a courier or a driver, and Grant's sister was the main earner."

"That's another thing. Jaime says he's never been married," Celeste said, lifting her coffee cup and swirling the dregs.

"Of course he'd tell that to a woman on a date."

"We already know Grant is lying about himself. Maybe he lied about his sister and Jaime."

"That would mean this whole job is a lie, and I'm getting played." Truman folded his arms. "That's totally possible."

"I'm glad you're open to the idea, at least."

"The first rule of detective work is: Don't believe anything that anybody says."

"Did you just make that up, or did you read it online?"

"It's in a library book," he said, and fished Biff Sturgis's guide out of his backpack, handing it to her.

Celeste grinned as she flipped through it, then gave it back and told him more about the day, more of what Jaime had said. Her words were animated, her eyes bright as she gestured for emphasis. This wasn't the bearing of someone on downers, Truman thought, watching her. Maybe Grant had been wrong about that.

No part of her story portrayed Jaime as anything more than decent and respectful—opening doors for her, letting her decide what they were going to do. Listening to her talk, Truman really hoped she wasn't falling for this guy.

Suddenly Celeste sat up, her eyes wide. "Christ, there he is," she said.

Truman followed her gaze to the street outside, catching a glimpse of a lanky guy walking past on the busy sidewalk, wearing the loose white shirt he'd seen in the photo from the pier.

"Did he see you?" Truman said.

"I don't think so—he didn't even glance in the window. I wonder if he's looking for me?"

"If he were, wouldn't he just text you? He must be up to something else." Truman stood up. "I'm going to tail him."

"Do you even know how to do that?" Celeste said, with a dubious frown.

"I read about it," he said. "Biff Sturgis has a whole chapter on how to conduct tails."

"He might spot you."

"It doesn't matter. He's never seen me before." Truman headed for the door.

"Be careful," she called after him.

Being careful is why he was broke, he thought, pushing out onto the sidewalk and scanning the street. He actually needed to be less careful. This kind of work demanded that he be bold. Not reckless, like following Maxine into someone else's house and getting chased into the metro, but bold. Maybe he needed to work on sorting out the difference.

Truman spotted the white shirt crossing the street half a block away, and jogged to make the light. Walking quickly, he was soon just a few paces behind the guy. Not very tall, Jaime walked with a bit of a strut—not so as to draw attention, but enough to make room for himself, to show the world he was comfortable taking up space in it.

Slowing his pace and reaching into his pants, Jaime pulled out his phone and held it to his ear. Truman got a little closer, trying to overhear, but he soon realized Jaime was speaking rapidly in Spanish. Why had Truman never learned the language, in a city of five million Latinos? It definitely hobbled him in this kind of research.

Jaime turned into a laneway behind an office building, and Truman followed, not breaking his stride. It was a surface parking lot, he realized, once he was in the middle of it. Jaime approached the attendant's booth, handing over a yellow stub. There had been lots of people on the sidewalk, but here it was just Truman and Jaime and two parking guys.

"Do you have your ticket, boss?" one of them asked Truman.

Waiting for the other attendant to find his keys in the cabinet mounted on the booth, Jaime glanced at Truman, his gaze indifferent, the ghost of a sneer curling his upper lip.

"Actually, I was trying to take a shortcut," Truman said, feeling his face heating up. He jutted his chin toward the back of the lot. "Does the alley go through to Eighth Street?"

"It does," the attendant said, "but I wouldn't advise it."

"Why not? It's broad daylight."

"Right, but you know how Skid Row doesn't have any toilets?"

"OK," Truman said. "I get it." Shoving his hands into his jacket pockets, he turned to walk back the way he'd come. As he reached the sidewalk, he glanced back to see Jaime getting into his ride. So that was the classic Road Runner. It looked fast. Of course this guy would drive a car like that, with big horsepower under the hood.

Walking back to the coffeehouse, he scanned the street before he went in. There was no sign of Jaime's distinctive wheels.

"Did you find him?" she asked, as Truman sat down across from her.

"I followed him into a parking lot," he said, and sipped at his now cold espresso. "He just got into that muscle car of his and left. I felt kind of stupid, walking in there when I don't have a car."

"Did he see you?"

"I was standing next to him—he looked right at me."

"Truman, you dizzy dolt—now you can't go talk to him. He'll know you were following him."

He watched her for a moment, thinking about it. "Why didn't I think of that?" he demanded.

"If I'd been able to get better intel, it wouldn't matter," she said. "Maybe he won't remember you in a day or two."

"Still, it was a stupid move." He folded his arms, angry with himself. Biff Sturgis would be very disappointed. "Maybe I'm not cut out for this kind of work."

"I disagree," she said. "You've already detected the guy, detective. From here it's just a little more effort. I have an in with him—I can do the talking."

"How are we going to do that?"

"I think he likes me," she said simply. "I'll take him on another date."

———◆———

After he slammed the last of his coffee, Truman walked to the station with Celeste, each of them descending onto different platforms, separated by the chasm of the rail bed. For the short time they waited for one of their trains to pull in, Celeste made faces at him, scowling and crossing her eyes, then grinning and grimacing like a goon. She had so much energy today. It got Truman laughing, and he boarded the train with a smile on his face.

ELEVEN

In the morning Truman woke to the scent of coffee, and rather than climbing back into bed, he stood in the patch of sunlight from the windows to sip at his steaming mug, shivering in the cold and letting the brightness of the day help wake him up.

There were things to do, and once he'd drained his cup, he got dressed and headed to the central library. After he'd returned his books—the ones about Boyle Heights, not Biff Sturgis's guidebook; he wasn't done with that one yet—he went down the stairs into the depths of the building and sought out the research counter. A woman with heavy blue eyeshadow, her dark hair pulled back, came over to talk to him.

"How can I check on a death record?" Truman

asked.

"Do you need a death certificate?"

"Just the basics, like the date."

"Well, if the person had a Social Security number, you could check the federal database," she said, and told him how to access it.

Truman pulled his pad out of his backpack and made notes. "What about marriage records?"

"Those go by county. For LA, you have to go to a county office."

"Where's that?"

"There are a few of them," she said, "but none of them are downtown."

"That makes absolutely no sense," Truman said sharply, meeting her eye.

She shrugged. "Bureaucracy is fickle. You'll need to be extremely patient."

After he wrote down what he had to look for, Truman went to a desk and pulled out his laptop. There was no one named Catherine Williams on the death rolls anywhere nearby in the last few years, no matter how he spelled the name. Maybe he had the time frame wrong. But even then, the most recent possibility was almost a decade ago, and even that Catherine didn't fit; she had been in her eighties.

Truman sat back and thought about it. It didn't necessarily mean Grant was lying. Maybe he was missing something. The marriage records might be more informative.

Based on where all the county offices were, scrolling around on a map, it was hard to decide which would be the least time-consuming of all the bad options. The librarian was right—he was going to need patience for this.

Packing up his computer and his notes, he went back up to the street and walked to the metro. He had to change trains in the middle of a freeway junction, concrete ramps arcing overhead and all around, watching the insanely loud traffic whiz by right next to the platform. From the station in Norwalk, the map on his phone said it was a fifty-minute walk to the county office, so he called a ride-share.

When he finally got there, stepping inside, he saw that the place was quiet, at least, with no one waiting at the counter, and no one visible behind it. As Truman approached, the clerk, sitting at a desk nearby, caught sight of him and stood up. He wore thick-framed glasses and had his hair done in neat little twist curls on top. It looked expensive, and time-consuming.

"How can I check on a marriage record?" Truman asked.

"Are you a party to the marriage or a direct relative?" the clerk asked, his tone perfunctory, boredom in his eyes.

"I just want to see the date it happened, that

kind of thing."

The guy slid a sheet of yellow paper across to him. It was a form, topped by the county seal, with a dozen boxes to be filled in. "Come back with a photo ID and fifteen dollars."

Truman sat in one of the hard plastic chairs and found a pen in his bag, which he set in his lap to write on. Moments later, stepping back to the counter, he slid the yellow page across, then dug out his driver's license and three fins as he waited for the clerk.

"You only filled in the names," the clerk said, frowning as he studied the sheet. He picked up Truman's license, compared it to what Truman had written at the bottom of the sheet, and handed the card to him.

"I don't know any of the other details. That's why I'm here."

"Well, if it's in the database, we'll find it," he said, scooping up the bills. "Informational copies are mailed out in about three weeks."

"Can't I get it now?"

The clerk shook his head. "No way."

"I don't actually need a copy of the document. All I need to know is whether they really were married."

The clerk folded his arms and frowned. "Three weeks," he said firmly.

"You said that already," Truman said flatly,

and stepped away, pulling on his backpack. Before he gave up, though, maybe he could try the technique the woman had taught him at the Highland Arms.

Digging in his pants pocket, he found a twenty and folded it up, making sure the number on the bill was visible, then palmed it, and went back to the counter.

"I forgot to ask you something," Truman said, evoking a scowl from the guy, who hauled himself up from his desk and stepped to the counter. "Is there an express fee just to check the database? I don't need anything printed out." He flashed the twenty in his palm, just long enough for the guy to see it.

The clerk glanced at his colleague, sitting at the next desk. She was ignoring them. "There's no express service."

"Still, you can check the records, right? It's just a yes-or-no thing. And maybe the date when they got married."

Hesitating for a moment, the clerk finally tapped Truman's hand, deftly claiming the twenty before he returned to his desk. Looking at the form Truman had written on, he typed and peered at his computer. Eventually he stood up again and leaned on the counter, holding Truman's gaze.

"I'm not seeing anybody with those names," he

said quietly. "At least not married to each other."

"That's all I needed," Truman said, and jutted his chin toward the desk. "Can I have that form back?"

He frowned but turned to pluck it from his desk, handing it to Truman.

The clerk hadn't copied Truman's ID or swiped it through a reader; he'd only compared it to what Truman had written. In Biff Sturgis's words, "Never leave behind evidence of your own work." This piece of paper had his name on it, and it was evidence that Truman had been snooping on Jaime, so it only made sense to reclaim it.

"What about the fifteen bucks?" Truman said, folding the sheet in half and tucking it into his backpack.

The guy just laughed. "So if a marriage isn't in our system, it doesn't mean they didn't get married in Vegas or Tijuana. Just not in LA."

"Good to know," Truman said.

Something in the clerk's demeanor had shifted, his expression softening. "Do you live around here?" he said. "There are some fun places to go out. It's almost closing time."

"I'm flattered," Truman said carefully, holding his gaze, "but I can't." Not waiting for a response, he turned to leave.

Interesting that bending the rules made the

clerk think they were on a more intimate footing, he thought, walking out toward the boulevard. The guy wasn't bad looking, but no way was he going to date a corrupt bureaucrat.

———◆———

That morning Celeste had slept in, happy not to have to go to work. She lay in bed for a while, dozing, thinking about her day out with Jaime. Everything about him said that he was boyfriend material. Was that a completely crazy notion? Of course it was. Even considering such a thing meant she was probably as deluded about guys as Truman.

When she finally got up and wandered into the kitchen, María was at the table.

"I'd offer you breakfast, but it's more like lunchtime," she said.

"I'll just have some fruit," Celeste said, and went to the espresso maker and switched it on.

"Can we split that?"

"Sure," Celeste said, and got out two demitasse cups.

"I wish I'd known it was your day off too. We could have planned something."

"It's nice to have a lazy morning, don't you think?"

"You look tired, *mija,*" María said, watching her work.

"I was in the sun a lot yesterday. Usually I'm in that gloomy gallery."

"Are you sure there isn't something else? I worry about you."

"I'm fine," Celeste said flatly. "There's nothing to worry about."

María folded her arms as Celeste set the demitasse cup in front of her. "I wish I could believe that."

"There is something you can help me with." Celeste sat across from her, holding her little cup in both hands, savoring its warmth. "Can you ask some of your friends about a guy I met? He's from the neighborhood. I want to know who his people are."

"Where did you meet him?"

"Downtown. His name is Jaime Martínez. I think he's connected to someone named Vanessa Martínez. I have her address. Give me a sec." Celeste went into her bedroom to retrieve the note Bibi had written, handing it to her.

"I know where that is," María said, glancing at the page. "Lots of people have that surname, but I'll ask around. What does this boy look like?"

Celeste described him, and María nodded thoughtfully, then rose. As she ate an apple and finished her coffee, Celeste could hear her chatting on the phone somewhere in the back of the house, her words indistinct with the distance.

Eventually Celeste got dressed and went out to do a couple of day-off errands. Sitting in her car in the parking lot after she hit the bank, she pulled out her phone and found the address Bibi had given her on a map. Whether Vanessa Martínez really lived there or not, it wasn't far away. Starting the engine, Celeste pulled onto the street and headed there.

The house was a tiny bungalow in the middle of a crowded block. The garage doors were closed, and the red work pickup Truman had described was sitting in the driveway, with the gate to the street rolled shut behind it. Cruising slowly past, the house itself revealed nothing. It was hard to believe that Truman had been tramping around inside it with some woman he'd just met.

When she pulled up in front of her own house again and went inside, María came into the front room and waggled her phone.

"I think I found your boyfriend," she said gleefully.

"That was fast." Celeste stepped into the kitchen and dropped her keys on the table. "And he's not my boyfriend."

"Vanessa is his mother. I don't think they live at this address anymore. You could ask her sister about that," María said. "I know her—Jaime's aunt. Her name is Tina. Back in the day, she and I worked on the same paper. A little community rag we set up during the protests."

"*¡Ya Basta!*" Celeste said, eliciting a chuckle from her mother. She knew vaguely that "back in the day" meant the 1980s, but she didn't want to hear about politics right now. "Do you have her phone number?"

"She runs a flower shop over by the school. Drop in and talk to her."

"Your network is amazing."

"It's all about community. Invest a little in it, and the payoff is huge."

Celeste hugged her, then said, "Where are my keys?"

"Kitchen table," María said, and smiled as Celeste grabbed them and hustled out.

———◆———

A few blocks from the county records office, Truman still couldn't find a bus stop. Surely there'd be a way to get to the metro without walking all the way. Everything was so spread out once you left the city. You really had to have wheels out here. Eventually he found an odd-looking bus stop with a logo he'd never seen before. A woman was standing nearby, and he spoke to her.

"Does this route go to the metro station?"

"That's all it does," she said, eyeing him. "If it ever comes."

Truman's phone buzzed in his pants, and he

stepped away to pull it out and check. It was Grant.

"I'm glad you called," Truman said. "We need to talk."

"Have you found Jaime?"

"I got close to him last night, and I'm working on reeling him in."

"Just tell me where to find him," Grant said. "I don't need anything more than that."

"I don't know that yet. Soon."

Grant sighed. "You're not stringing me along, are you?"

"Don't stress about the money, if that's what you're getting at," Truman said, thinking quickly. "I'm not going to charge you for full days. I'm thinking I've worked two half days since Monday."

"I don't care about the cost, but I would like a status report."

"I just told you where things stand. I'm really close."

"I meant in person."

"Right," Truman said, suddenly understanding. "I'd be happy to see you, but it won't be soon. I'm fifty minutes' walk past the ass end of nowhere."

"I'll be home in an hour."

The woman waiting with him stepped toward the curb, and Truman saw a little shuttle bus approaching, its blinker on as it pulled to the curb.

"I'll see you there," he told Grant.

Celeste knew the retail strip that her mother had been talking about, and even had a vague memory of the flower shop. Driving past, she saw that the place was open, and parked around the corner.

The storefront wasn't very wide, but inside there was lots of inventory, brightly colored blooms arrayed in buckets, on tables, and inside a cold room with big glass doors. A bell tinkled overhead as she stepped in from the street, and from the back a woman appeared. She was María's age, tall and wiry, her short hair pushed behind her ears. There was a resemblance to Jaime, maybe, in the shape of her face, the line of her brow.

"Are you Tina?" she asked. "I'm Celeste."

"María's daughter. You look a lot like her." She smiled, giving Celeste the once-over, creases forming at the corners of her eyes. "It's like a time warp, seeing her the way she looked at your age."

"She talked about a newsletter. You worked on it together?"

Tina nodded. "We were organizing the community. Your mother was a bad-ass with a megaphone."

Celeste laughed. "I wish I'd seen that."

"Ask her for photos. I'm sure she has some. I know Neto as well."

"Was my father around then too?" she said, forcing a smile. Talking about her parents seemed like a waste of time.

"He worked with us a lot. I remember him as a guy who always showed up when you asked him to. Your mother is the one who would get everyone fired up and chanting the same slogan. Your father is the one who would paint the signs, or help you get your cat out of a tree."

Celeste nodded. "That does sound like them. It's hard to imagine them as agitators, though."

"A better word is 'activists,'" she said, and put her hands on her hips. "So you wanted to know about Jaime. Are you sweet on him?"

"Not really," Celeste said, blushing. "I just went out with him once. He said he was from the neighborhood."

"He was a good kid," Tina said, raising her eyebrows.

"Was?" Celeste demanded.

"He got mixed up with some rough people. That doesn't mean he's a bad person, just that he's doing stupid things."

Celeste frowned. "He doesn't seem like a gangbanger."

"If it was just the neighborhood yahoos, it would be easier to pull him out of it. Unfortunately his employers are far worse than that."

"Who does he work for?"

"You should talk that through with him. I already feel like a gossip."

"OK," she said, and sighed impatiently, absently scratching her arm. "Does he live with Vanessa? I know she was over on Oakwood."

"Vanessa moved out of that house a while back. He definitely doesn't stay with her. She's afraid to have him around."

"Seriously?" From his own mother that seemed extreme, no matter what his job was. "So where does he stay?"

"No idea," Tina said, raising her eyebrows. "I don't want to butt into your business, but the last thing I'll say is that Jaime doesn't have a great reputation with women."

The bell over the door tinkled, and Celeste turned to see a guy walking in. She scowled at the interruption.

Tina greeted him in Spanish, then said to Celeste, "Do me a favor—take your mother some flowers."

"That's very generous," Celeste said, and watched her deftly pluck stems from the bins. Clearly Tina wasn't going to spill any other details about Jaime. The customer was looking around toward the back of the store, out of earshot. "If you don't mind, don't mention to Jaime that I came to see you. I didn't tell him my real name."

Tina nodded, tying twine around the bouquet

she'd created. "That's so smart. And don't worry—I never see him anyway."

Climbing into her car, Celeste set the newspaper-wrapped bouquet on the seat. That had been annoying, but not entirely fruitless. Tina was nice enough; why was Celeste so irked by it all? It struck her then—it had been a while since she'd taken a Vicodin.

"You're not an addict," she said aloud, digging in the center console until she found one, biting it in half and grinding it in her teeth. She grimaced at the bitterness. It was just for maintenance, to smooth her irritation, even things out. When she'd been without it for a while, she got kind of antsy like this. But that didn't make her an addict. She started the engine and pulled out, phoning Truman as she drove home.

When he picked up, she said, "Where are you? It sounds like you're standing on the side of the freeway."

"I am, literally—I'm at a station in the middle of the 105."

"So I met Jaime's aunt. There's stuff to fill you in on. Do you want to grab dinner?"

"I can't," Truman said. "I've got a meeting."

"Drinks later, then. How about that place on Seventh with the plaid carpet?"

"Sure, but what did the aunt say about Jaime?"

"Vanessa is Jaime's mother, so Bibi found

the right vehicle. But the address on the title is a dud—she moved out of that house a while ago."

"So my prowling and trespassing were completely pointless," Truman said.

"The aunt doesn't know where Jaime lives, but he doesn't stay with Vanessa anymore—she's afraid of him."

"Why?"

"She said the people he works for are bad news. I couldn't really press her to say who they were, but the implication was clear."

"He's a gangster?"

"Not like a street gang, she told me. But she implied that he works for some bad people."

"Seriously?" Truman said. It wasn't surprising, not really, but hearing her say it, having it confirmed, made his pulse quicken.

"I find it so hard to believe," Celeste said. "He's just so ordinary."

"I wish this job was over with already," Truman said, raising his voice to be heard over the traffic. "I was doing research today too. There's no death record for Grant's sister, and Jaime was never married to her. I'm not sure she's real."

"I knew it," Celeste said emphatically.

"It's also possible that I got the name wrong. Or maybe they got married outside LA County and never reported it."

"We know Grant is lying about other stuff.

The simplest explanation is that he's lying about his sister."

"It looks that way," Truman said, and it fit with Biff Sturgis's first rule of detective work: Don't believe anything that anybody says. "That doesn't mean Jaime is on the up-and-up either, especially if his aunt says he's a crook."

"I get that, Truman," she said, raising her voice. "We'll talk about it later."

The line went dead, and Truman looked at his phone to make sure she really had hung up on him. Tucking his phone away, he stepped toward the train as it pulled in, and boarded with the throng of other riders.

Celeste wasn't being objective about the guy at all—she was totally crushing on him. Jaime was a lowlife, he knew that now. Grant hadn't exactly lied about everything—he said Jaime was a courier, which fit with what Jaime himself had told Celeste. The only thing the aunt had added was that he worked for crooks. But Grant had lied about so many other things, including his relationship to Jaime.

Hanging onto the pole as the train swayed, Truman felt a queasy lump in his stomach. Biff never mentioned that part of the work: physical symptoms of the burgeoning fear and dread. Truman knew for certain now that he was being played. He was out of his depth with these people.

TWELVE

The loud red boat of a car was in the drive-way when Truman walked up on Grant's house an hour later. Grant flashed that beautiful smile when he opened the door.

"My favorite detective," he said.

"How many detectives do you know?" Truman said, stepping inside.

"Out of all of them, you're the hottest."

Truman wanted to ask how many booty-call partners Grant actually had, but when he thought about it, he didn't really want to know.

Grant's clothes were mostly off by the time they got to his bed, and he pushed Truman down, straddling him, leaning down to kiss him, his mouth hot and insistent. Running his hands under Truman's shirt, Grant sighed with pleasure, pulling it off and then unbuckling Truman's belt. Grant grabbed his cock, stroking it until he was rock hard, their mouths locked together. Soon Truman was close to him, his arms wrapped around his chest, and then inside him. Grant groaned with the intensity of it, their bodies rocking together.

Afterward, Truman stretched out on his back. Grant put his arm across his chest and nuzzled his neck.

"So where's Jaime?" Grant said softly. "If you found him, how hard can it be to explain it to me?"

"I found his ex-girlfriend," Truman said, "and I tailed her to get a bead on the guy. I just need to find out where he's staying."

"Or just tell me where he hangs out."

"I don't know that either. You need to have some patience, man."

"And you need to nut up," Grant said, pulling back. "I'm not paying you again until you deliver."

"Fine," Truman said flatly. "Where did he and your sister get married?"

"Does it matter?"

"It might be useful."

"They never told me," Grant said. "They might not have done it legally, although they told me they did. And if you've already found the guy, how would that information help?"

"How long were they together?"

Grant moved his big hand to Truman's neck, gripping firmly under his jaw. It wasn't so tight as to cut off his air, but the threat was clear. "Truman, just do your damn job. Quit dicking around."

Truman took hold of his wrist, slowly pulling his hand away, and turned toward him. His heart was pounding. Those weren't unreasonable questions, and the story was changing—the guy was definitely lying. But this wasn't the time to get into it, not if Grant was going to throttle him. Gently putting a hand on Grant's cheek, he said, "Chill," and kissed him, lingering in it, using it to shift his focus.

Eventually Grant sat up. "Do you want to eat?"

"I have to go," Truman said, and got up and went into the bathroom to wash up.

After he was dressed, he found Grant standing in the kitchen, still naked, eating out of a black takeout container.

"You sure you're not hungry?" Grant said, gesturing with a forkful of something fried. "There's lots."

Truman studied his face. The guy was pretty glib for someone who had just physically threatened him. He kissed him good-bye and then headed out to the dark street.

On the walk back to the metro in Hollywood, he thought things through. There was no sister, he was sure of that now. He wasn't going to sleep with Grant again either—it wasn't safe. Should he deliver Jaime anyway? To figure that out, he needed to talk to Celeste.

———•———

Pausing to show his ID to the bouncer at the door, Truman trotted up the plaid-carpeted stairs to the dimly lit interior of the bar. The place was styled like a hunting lodge, complete with stomach-churning taxidermy on the walls, but the drinks were relatively cheap, and it was close to the metro.

Celeste was on a stool at the crowded bar, he saw as he walked in, wearing a low-cut blouse and talking to a guy, standing beside her, in jeans and a leather jacket. As he approached them, Truman stopped short. The guy she was with was Jaime. What the hell?

Celeste caught sight of him and waved him over. Truman hesitated, but then took a deep breath and approached them.

"This is my friend Truman," she said, raising her voice over the music and the loud conversations around them in the bar. "Truman, this is Jaime."

Jaime grinned at him, his eyes bright, and gestured with the beer bottle he held in his hand. "Apologies for crashing your night out."

"No worries," Truman said affably, watching Jaime's face for any flicker of recognition. Maybe he'd forgotten about seeing Truman in the parking lot.

"Penelope said she was meeting her bestie, and I thought I should tag along."

"I'm happy to meet you," Truman said, and shot Celeste a quizzical look.

But Celeste was focused on the black-shirted bartender, and was leaning toward him across the bar to be heard. "A blended margarita for my friend here," she said.

"I'm so glad you're gay," Jaime said. "It means I don't have to be all competitive."

"Not that we're gossiping or anything," Truman said, and glared at Celeste, who just shrugged.

Jaime laughed. "How do you know Penelope?"

"We were at school together. We used to collaborate on cooking up ways to get out of PE. How did you two meet?"

"It was like I had a vision," Jaime said. "I got one look at her and just could not tear my eyes away."

That was an evasive answer, Truman thought. But maybe he was just trying to be gallant, rather than explaining that she'd picked him up in a dive bar. Hearing him say it, Celeste beamed.

"So what do you do?" Jaime asked.

"I'm mostly a tour guide."

"Like on those open buses on Hollywood Boulevard?"

Truman gestured with a flourish and spoke with his methodical tour-guide diction. "On the left is the front gate of a big house you can't see. It belongs to a big actor you'll never see either."

Jaime laughed. "That sounds pretty dry."

"I do history tours too. Those are more fun."

The bartender set down his margarita, icy green, the rim sparkling with salt. Truman dug in his pocket for cash, but Jaime had already pulled out his billfold. Pulling off a twenty, he set it on the bar top, and the bartender grabbed it and stepped away.

"Thanks, man," Truman said, and reached for the drink.

Jaime grinned and met his eye, rearranging the wad of paper that had come out of his pocket with the cash.

Celeste clinked her bottle on Truman's glass. "I was on my way here when Jaime called. He was downtown too. I figured it was a good opportunity for you two to meet."

"More people, more fun, right?" Truman said. "What do you do, Jaime?"

"Gig work." He shrugged, tucking his billfold back in his pants and crumpling up the rest of the paper in his fist, dropping the rumpled ball on the counter beside Celeste's drink. "Courier, driver, that kind of thing. Have you been to Penelope's gallery?"

Truman nodded. "Many times. It's like a crypt down there. The art is really vapid and trashy. It makes me sad."

"Art is subjective," Celeste said, waving a hand. "A piece that Truman thinks is bad art is what someone else is willing to shell out fifty grand for."

"I guess at those prices you can afford for the place to sit empty," Jaime said. "You only need a few whales, not a bunch of small fish."

"It really just proves that rich and stupid aren't mutually exclusive," Truman said, and sipped his drink. "How many times have I looked at pieces in there and said, 'A nine-year-old could have done that'? Or I could have, with a free afternoon and ten bucks' worth of art supplies."

"But the key point," Celeste said intently, "is that you didn't."

"I can see you two have history," Jaime said, and looked at Celeste. "It's great to have friends."

"You don't?" she asked.

"Sure I do, but not many that I trust." He casually put his arm on her back and looked to Truman. "So what do you call her as a nickname? Penny?"

"Pen-Pen," Truman said flatly.

"I like that," Jaime said.

Celeste scowled. "I don't. Sometimes I call him Tru, but it doesn't really fit his personality."

Jaime laughed and took a swig of beer.

"I'll be back," Celeste said, and slid off her stool.

Truman sat in her place to save it, his back to the bar, and eyed Jaime. "So you two just met."

"That's right. We went to the beach yesterday, and had a pizza."

"What's the attraction? Is she your type physically, or is it something about her personality?"

"I don't know, man. I like all kinds of women. And I really like her."

"It seems fast," Truman said. "I'm not telling you what to do, but I wonder if you should pace yourself. You know, slow things down. Cool your jets."

Jaime's eyes went hard, and he stuck out his chin. "Don't you worry about what I'm doing. You keep out of my business, and you won't get hurt."

Truman felt his heart start to pound, felt his face go red. But he held Jaime's gaze—he wasn't going to be intimidated. As Biff Sturgis said, "Don't let the chumps see you sweat."

"I'm not messing with you, Jaime," Truman said. "I don't even know you."

"Good answer," he said, still glaring, and took a swig from his bottle.

Celeste came back, and Truman stood for her to take the stool.

"I've got a work thing," Jaime said, "but I

wanted to see your lovely face." Leaning in, he kissed her on the mouth, lingering for a moment.

Celeste looked surprised but went with it, closing her eyes.

"I'll call you," Jaime said, setting his bottle on the bar. Meeting Truman's eye with a cool gaze, he added, "Bye, Truman."

Truman watched him leave before he spoke. "What the hell was that?" he demanded. "Dude could have made me from last night."

"But he didn't," she said. "And I didn't spill anything. I figured you could talk your way out of it"—she frowned and spoke in a deep voice, mimicking him—"'Yeah, I was in that parking lot; what a coincidence. I walk around there all the time.' Besides, I thought maybe you'd tell him about Grant."

"I'm glad you didn't, at least."

"It's your gig, so that's your call," she said, and reached for her beer.

Her eyelids were drooping, Truman realized, and when she blinked, they seemed a little slow. Was her judgment impaired? It wasn't the beer— she couldn't have been drinking for very long.

"Are you on something?" he asked.

She scowled. "Why would you say that?"

"Grant says you're on opiates."

"Grant should mind his own damn business. You already know he's a liar."

"Do not lie to me," Truman said, raising his voice. "Everyone on this job is lying about everything. If you're lying too, I'll lose sight of the ground, lose contact with reality. I've known you for too long, Pen-Pen."

"Don't call me that," she snapped. "You know what? You've fallen for that guy."

"Bullshit," Truman said. "And that's just what I was going to say to you."

"You're talking crazy," she said intently.

"Maybe," Truman said, and looked away. He was a little buzzed from the tequila, and willed himself to be calm. "I'm not especially attached to being considered sane."

Celeste stared at him. "Do you think we're codependent?"

"Meaning what?"

"If I didn't hang around with you so much, maybe we'd both get boyfriends."

"I introduced you to your last boyfriend."

"He was a dud."

Truman gestured with his glass, the icy dregs sloshing in the bottom. "How is that my fault? Get a grip, woman. You can meet guys without me around."

"Excellent idea," Celeste said, and slid off her stool, then walked to the stairs.

Truman sat in her place, watching her go, stunned at how quickly that had happened. He'd hurt her feelings, he realized, and that made him feel a twinge of guilt. Maybe he shouldn't have asked whether she was on drugs. But it was telling that she hadn't denied it.

Setting his glass on the bar top, he saw that the little wad of crumpled paper Jaime had left was still sitting there with the bottles. He pulled it apart to find that it comprised several cards from automated parking lots and a couple of receipt stubs from valets. They didn't seem insightful—on heavy pink or yellow or white paper, they were all generic, with the name of the provider and a boilerplate legal disclaimer in tiny print on the back, and none of them identified a specific location.

But as he flattened them out, among the cards was a bit of cash-register tape, hazy heat-printed lettering on thin white paper. Across the top it was inscribed PALETAS HERNÁN, with an address in Huntington Park. The slip was dated today, but he couldn't make out anything below that line, the sensitive paper creased and darkened with wear.

A bar back stopped and grabbed the empties. Leaving all the rumpled parking cards on the bar, Truman slid the receipt into his pants pocket and headed for the stairs.

———◆———

Once he got home, he stretched out on the most comfortable of the sofas with his laptop. *Paletas,* according to the Spanish-English translation site, meant wooden pallets, used in shipping and in warehouses. Looking at Paletas Hernán on the map, it was a storefront on a busy retail strip, on a block with a cell-phone outlet, a shop called Beauty Supply, and a place for *tacos al vapor.* It didn't look like there'd be room for pallets, but maybe they just brokered them and didn't need space to store them or maneuver a forklift around. Whatever the case, if Jaime had been there, it was worth looking into.

Next Truman spent some time making notes, and thinking through what had happened today. His loyalty should be to the guy who was paying him, he knew that, even without checking in the *Hard-Nosed Detective* guide. But he might not get paid anyway—besides grabbing his throat, Grant had said as much tonight.

If he couldn't pin down an address for Jaime, the next logical step was to set up a meeting between them. It would be simple—Jaime would show up anywhere Celeste told him to. But before he did that, he wanted to confront Grant with all the lies, and try to get the real story. Had he really not expected Truman to figure out that he was lying? A flash of anger made him clench his teeth, realizing that Grant had underestimated him in that way. His next meeting with Grant would have to happen out somewhere, a bar or a restaurant, with witnesses, where he wouldn't get strangled, and far from the heater in Grant's sock drawer.

Checking the time, he saw that it was well after one. How had it gotten so late? He folded the computer closed and got up to prep the coffeemaker, setting the timer and then killing the lights and climbing into bed.

Jaime was an aggressive dick too, threatening him like that tonight, but it still wasn't right to turn him over to Grant without knowing why he was doing it. Rolling onto his back, Truman gazed up at the dark windows and sighed. The worst part was that confronting Grant increased the likelihood that he wasn't going to make any more money on this job.

THIRTEEN

The gurgling of the coffee machine woke Truman, and the aroma put a smile on his face as he padded across the cold floor to pour himself a mug. Grabbing his laptop, he climbed back into the warmth of his bed and plotted a route to Huntington Park.

Paletas Hernán was twenty-five minutes' walk from the metro station, which put it right in the ambiguous zone of whether waiting for a connecting bus would take longer than hoofing it. He'd walk, he decided. It was cold but it wasn't going to rain today. Forcing himself out of bed, he quickly got dressed and headed for the train.

The boulevard leading from the station was lined with industrial-scale warehouses, but once he got to the cross-street with the retail strip, there were more people around. Walking into Paletas Hernán, he quickly realized he'd been mistaken—it was an ice cream store, with rows of colorful popsicles on display behind the glass counter, not a pallet or a forklift in sight. The clerk was a dark-complected guy in a white apron, tufts of gray hair poking out around his little white soda-jerk cap, his face lined by time and laboring in the sun.

When the door chimed, the guy called out a perfunctory greeting in Spanish, but once he got a look at Truman stepping in, he said, "What'll it be, son?"

"So you sell ice cream," Truman said, frowning and surveying the case.

"None of these are ice cream. It's all fresh-fruit popsicles, handmade on-site."

"So why is the shop called Paletas?"

The clerk stared at him for a moment. "That's what we sell. These are *paletas*. *Paletas* means 'popsicles.'"

"Of course it does," Truman said, and sighed. He needed a better translation site. Jaime had probably just dropped in for a snack. Coming all the way down here was a waste of time.

"People really like the strawberry," the clerk said.

"Do you sell a lot of these in the winter?"

"You'd be surprised," he said flatly.

"Do you know a guy named Jaime Martínez?" Truman said, meeting his gaze.

His eyes narrowed. "Is he a friend of yours?"

"In a way."

The guy scoffed, and raised his voice. "Is he trying to bleed me dry, sending his people in here?" He stepped away and slammed the top of the display case closed. Before Truman could say anything, he added, "The best I can do is five for forty."

"OK," Truman said, watching him. Just the mention of Jaime's name had shifted this guy's whole demeanor into a state of agitation. "Forty … dollars?"

"That's what I said," he snapped. "I can do six, but you're ripping me off. How does Jaime expect any upstream growth when he's shaving my balls like this?"

"Let's do five, then, if six is unreasonable," Truman said. He had no idea what the guy was selling him, but for forty bucks, it wasn't popsicles.

"Let's see some cash," he demanded.

Truman dug in his pocket and handed him two twenties. The guy snatched them and pushed through the swinging door into the back, muttering under his breath.

So Jaime was known here. Scanning the place, there were a couple of narrow tables where people could sit to eat their icy snacks, deserted this early in the day. The popsicles looked fresh, and the lighted board above, with all the flavors listed in Spanish, showed the prices for all of them at just a dollar or two. Curiously, unlike most retail joints, there were no cameras mounted anywhere.

When the clerk returned, he had a white paper sack in hand, folded over at the top. Wordlessly, he handed it across the counter. It was as light as air. Maybe it was empty. Truman started to pull open the sack.

"You don't do that in here," the clerk shouted. "You don't get to distrust me. Goddamn junkie. Get the hell out."

"Fine," Truman said, frowning and backing toward the door.

"Tell Jaime to stop sending his junkie trash," he shouted after him. "He's not the only one who can prance around with a *pistola*."

Pushing through the door and breathing hard, Truman walked fast, back the way he'd come. He slid his backpack off and stuffed the white sack inside. Whatever it was could wait.

———·———

Once he was in his loft, with the door locked, Truman dropped onto the purple sofa and pulled open his backpack. Inside the paper sack was a little plastic zip-top bag with five delicate powder-blue packets inside, neatly folded in half. He didn't have to open them to know what it was: heroin. Not wanting to examine the sack in view of the cameras on the train, on the way home he'd basically worked it out—Truman had been called plenty of things, but "junkie trash" was a new one.

So Jaime was mixed up with drug dealers, and if the popsicle guy was to be believed, he packed a heater. He took a deep breath. Celeste was going to be pissed.

But first, what to do with this stuff? He studied the little envelopes, holding their container up to the light from the windows. There was definitely a thick uneven lump inside each of them. Truman was never going to use it, and he certainly wasn't going to resell it. Just having it could get him arrested. He got up and went to the bathroom, where he shook the packets into the toilet and flushed. He crumpled up the white sack and threw it in the garbage. That junk was much safer in the sewer than lying around his pad.

After he washed his hands, washed away whatever germs and drug residue were on that sack, he decided he couldn't put off making the call any longer, and dropped onto the sofa. Celeste picked up after a couple of rings.

"I'm sorry I upset you last night," Truman said.

"It's all right. It was an intense kind of evening."

"I didn't mean to hurt your feelings."

"I know. It's just that you're supposed to be

my friend—without judgment."

"I am," Truman said. "I'm not judging you. We should talk about it, but not on the phone. I was kind of blindsided to see my target there with you."

"It seemed like a good idea at the time," she said. "I thought you'd see that he's not such a bad guy."

Truman stifled his retort. Now was not the time to talk about bad judgment. "He wasn't there for very long."

"You weren't ready to come clean with him?" Celeste said.

"That wasn't my plan."

"But you're trying to wrap things up, right? I talked to Jaime today. He's on his way to San Diego for a few days and wanted to see me first. You'll love this—I had a brainwave and told him to pick me up at my cousin's house, but I gave him Grant's address."

"What?" Truman demanded, sitting up. His heart started to pound.

"It's a perfect solution—you don't have to track down where Jaime's staying, Grant gets what he's paying you for, and neither one of us has to be there in the middle of it."

"I wish you hadn't done that," Truman said. "This is my case."

"Sure, but I'm the one who wrangled Jaime."

"What if Grant is planning to mess him up? I

wanted to talk to him first, and make sure I wasn't putting Jaime in danger."

"Jaime is street smart," Celeste said. "Way more than fancy-pants Grant, and no offense, way more than you. He can take care of himself."

"I'm sure he can," Truman said, and sighed. Telling her what he'd learned about Jaime today would have to wait. "Can you call him off?"

"Why? Think about it, Truman. This way you can be done with it. Go over there tomorrow and collect the rest of your fee."

"Just stop him," Truman said. "It's important."

"He'll think I'm a weirdo."

"Make up some excuse," Truman said, and hung up.

———•———

Sitting at her desk in the empty gallery, Celeste sighed and stared absently into the cavernous space. Truman was overthinking this. She'd thought he'd be happy. Dialing Jaime's number, she got his voice mail.

"I have to postpone," she told the machine. "Call me before you come over."

Next she dialed Truman again.

"I couldn't get hold of him," she said, "but I left him a message."

"What time is he supposed to be there?"

"I told him four."

"Call me if you talk to him," Truman said, and the line went dead.

———◦———

Jumping up off the sofa, Truman hurriedly slung on his backpack. What was Celeste thinking? Jaime was street smart, sure, and Grant was slick, but they were both dangerous. No way was Truman going to be responsible for getting them together. Twisting his key in the deadbolt, he called a ride-share and headed down to the curb.

Waiting for the car, he thought it through. Regardless of how Jaime was related to Grant, if he actually knew him, maybe he'd recognize the address Celeste had given him and not even show up. But Grant had just moved there; Jaime wouldn't know he lived in that house. If Truman tried to intercept Jaime before he got there, the guy would probably just punch him in the face, no matter what he said. Maybe he could talk to Grant before the guy arrived.

His ride pulled up, and Truman climbed in and greeted the driver, a dark-haired woman in a denim jacket. A little card inscribed with Chinese characters hung from her rearview mirror by a red string.

"There's a sawbuck in it for you if you step on it," Truman said, remembering what Biff Sturgis said about motivating people.

"Not worth it to me, man," she said. "The software monitors my speed. If I want to keep working, I have to behave."

Truman folded his arms and looked out the window as she made her way to the freeway, then headed toward Hollywood. Maybe Truman could be there when Jaime arrived, and supervise the meeting, keep an eye on things, make sure nobody got hurt. He scoffed under his breath. Who was he kidding? No way could he slow either one of them down. The only thing he could do was talk to Grant before Jaime showed up—if Truman ever got there at these plodding law-abiding speeds— and hope that Celeste could intercept him.

Pulling out his phone, he texted her:

Any luck?

The driver exited the freeway onto Melrose. That's not the way Truman would have chosen, but hopefully her software knew something he didn't. He watched her charm card drift and flutter on its string, silently willing the vehicle to go faster, and looked at his phone again when it buzzed with Celeste's reply:

Nothing yet. What's going on?

Truman thumb-typed a terse response:

If you talk to him, don't spill the beans. More later.

The driver dropped him on Sunset, at the end of Grant's street. The oversize red car wasn't there, he saw, walking up on the house, and the sheers were drawn. Ringing the bell, he stood and listened, but there was no sound of movement from within. Maybe he could phone Grant, he thought, glancing around at the quiet street, or just wait on the front step for Jaime.

But he already knew how to get inside. That would be trespassing, or burglary, or something similarly unquestionably illegal, the kind of rash and reckless behavior that got him chased into the metro. He knew how Biff Sturgis would frame it, though. Truman had been in this house many times, and arguably Grant had given him the keys by not concealing the entry code from him—even if he got caught, he might be able to talk his way out of a charge.

Just to have a quick look around, he told himself, and then he'd wait outside for Jaime, try to stop the meeting that way. Typing the code on the electronic lock, the deadbolt slid open, and he pushed his way inside, closing the door behind him. He typed the code into the beeping alarm panel, silencing it, and then armed it again. Not knowing exactly how those things worked, it seemed wise to put it back the way it was. Truman stood there for a moment, listening to the house, but there was only silence.

Poking his head into Grant's room, the bed was unmade, and laundry was strewn on the floor. When Truman had been invited over, it was always much tidier. Grant hadn't been expecting guests today. In the second bedroom he saw there was a small pile of paper on the desk, and he stepped over to it, hesitant to snoop. But he was already on the wrong side of propriety. It was just mail, he found, flipping through it—a phone bill, an unopened bank statement, advertising.

Out front, he heard the sound of tires crunching on cement. Dropping the stack of mail, he hustled to the front room and looked through the sheers. The big red car was pulling into the driveway. Grant was home, and Truman was about to get busted.

Calm down, he told himself, taking deep breaths. Could he go out the kitchen door? Grant would see him, as it was within view of the front entrance, and how would he get out of the backyard? Maybe he could undress, and jump in the guy's bed, and play it coy. But that wouldn't change the fact that he'd broken in. Grant was typing his code into the door lock, Truman could hear it. Hustling into the guest bathroom, he pulled open the cactus-covered shower curtain and hopped into the bathtub, whipping the curtain across again as the front door opened.

If Grant came in here, he was sunk. But he wouldn't—no one had ever used this tub. Grant was at the alarm now, typing his code into it. His phone, he remembered. If that started ringing, he'd definitely get caught. Truman pulled it out and silenced it, gingerly sliding it back into his pants, trying not to make a sound.

Grant was moving around the house. First came the distinct clatter of keys on the kitchen counter, and then the sound of water briefly running in the adjacent sink. If he leaned on the wall at the end of the tub, Truman could see through the gap around the curtain into the living room, but Grant wasn't in view. Still in the kitchen, he realized, hearing the refrigerator door.

How long could Truman stand here without making a noise and giving himself away? There was room to stretch out, if he wanted to; he could even sleep. But if Grant was in for the evening, he needed to come up with an exit plan.

The chime of the doorbell interrupted his thoughts. That had to be Jaime—and Truman was trapped in here, unable to do anything about it. He leaned on the wall and peered into the front room. Grant didn't walk toward the front door, although he could hear his footsteps, and then heard the sound of a drawer sliding open. His pulse quickened when he realized what he was doing. Grant was in his sock drawer.

A moment later Grant walked past the bathroom, now on his way to the front door. Truman caught a glimpse of the heater, shoved in his belt in the small of his back, just above those perfect buttocks. Grant had never pulled a gun on Truman when he rang the doorbell, but then again, Truman had never shown up unexpected.

Truman couldn't see the front door, but he heard it open, and then heard Jaime's voice.

"What the fuck?" Jaime demanded.

"Come on in, stranger," Grant said. "This is a surprise, but I'm happy to see you."

"Don't point that thing at me."

The heater, Truman realized. He was aiming it at Jaime. Blood pounded in his ears.

Jaime stepped into view, wearing his leather jacket, his hands casually held up at his sides.

"Sit down," Grant demanded, walking behind him with the weapon in his hand, leveled at Jaime's torso.

Jaime slowly pulled a chair out from the dining table and sat, showing his palms again at chest height. He was breathing hard, and the look on his face was raw hatred. Grant positioned himself with his back to the bathroom, but Truman still had a view of Jaime, and of the ugly weapon in Grant's hand.

"Are you packing?" Grant said.

"My piece is in my car. I should have realized

that shit-box Caddy wasn't hers. Why didn't that click?"

"It's not a shit-box," Grant said, raising his voice.

"I was always the guy with the classic car," Jaime said, his lip curling into a sneer. "It was my look. You copied that from me."

"Shut up about my car," Grant demanded.

"I can't believe she set me up. Is she working for you, or your friends down south?"

"Who are you talking about?"

"Penelope—she told me to come here."

"Penelope?" Grant said, gesturing with the gun.

"Curvy Latina with long hair," Jaime said, frowning at him.

"Right." Grant nodded. "You never did have a clue about women. They always ran circles around you."

Jaime looked away. "You're right about that."

"In her defense," Grant said, "she didn't know she was setting you up."

"Then why did she send me here?"

"I'm not sure. She definitely didn't know the nature of our business relationship. You know, at one point I wondered if she was a junkie. Hanging around with you, that wouldn't be a surprise. Still, that's pretty low, getting your girlfriend hooked on smack."

"Would you stop pointing that thing at me?" Jaime said sharply. "You're making me nervous. Let's just talk things through."

"That ship has sailed," Grant said.

"I know what you're thinking. It's not that simple. Just—hear me out."

"If you knew what I was thinking, *cholo*, you'd be afraid. Very afraid."

Truman shifted his weight from one foot to the other, his calves sore from standing in the narrow space. Was he about to witness a murder? There was nothing he could do about it—if he showed himself now, tried to derail whatever was about to happen, Grant might shoot him too.

"Listen," Jaime said, squirming in the chair. "There's some cash in my car. I'm due to connect with the shipping people in San Diego tonight. Let me walk out of here, and the money is yours."

"After what you did to me?" Grant said, his voice rising. "Your life is not for sale."

"It's a lot of dough, Grant. Business has been good."

"Thank you for telling me about it. Are you still driving that stupid Road Runner?"

Jaime's eyes went dead, and he looked away.

Grant stepped out of view, and Truman watched Jaime's head turn, his gaze following Grant as he stepped into the kitchen. A drawer opened, cutlery rattled, and Grant reappeared, tossing something shiny toward Jaime, who caught it in one hand. A pair of handcuffs.

"Put that on your right wrist," Grant said, and waited while Jaime complied.

Truman heard the cuffs click as the locking mechanism engaged, and Jaime held up his hand, the other cuff dangling from his wrist.

"Hold your hands behind the chair," Grant said. "If you move an inch, I'll ventilate you."

Jaime dropped his hands behind his back, his face a mask of defeat. Grant stepped behind the chair and stooped down, followed by the click of the other cuff taking hold.

Rising, Grant shoved the heater in the back of his belt again and knelt in front of Jaime, groping his jacket pockets, then his pants. When he stood again he had a set of keys in his hand. Stepping into the kitchen, Truman heard him scoop up his own keys. Crossing his field of view again, Grant headed toward the front door.

"Don't go anywhere," Grant said, and went out, closing the door behind him.

Jaime immediately tried to stand up, but Grant had cuffed him to the chair, and he couldn't get his balance, and collapsed into it. He tried again, throwing himself upward, shifting the chair an inch or so. Outside the Cadillac's tires crunched on the gritty driveway. Was Grant leaving?

Truman stayed in the bathtub, watching

Jaime around the edge of the curtain, paralyzed in his own predicament. Should he step out and try to help the guy? Jaime was heaving the chair around now, moving it a few inches on the carpet each time. But Truman had no way to get him out of the cuffs or out of that chair. Call the cops, he realized. That's what he could do. Why hadn't he thought of that as soon as Grant left?

But before he could reach for his phone, Grant came back in, slamming the door behind him, and Truman froze. Peering out into the living room again, he saw Grant was carrying a black duffel bag. Jaime stopped squirming and watched him. Grant dropped the bag on the carpet and zipped it open, then let out a low whistle.

"This really is a fuck-ton of cash," Grant said. "I'm half tempted to keep this, and let the boys from the other side of the border take you out for bungling the delivery."

"Great idea," Jaime said, holding his gaze. "You keep the dough, and let me go explain it to them."

"The problem is, that wouldn't be very satisfying for me."

"Think about it, Grant—even if you ice me, they'll know you took the shipment. They won't let it go."

"You won't need to worry about that," Grant said, and zipped the bag closed.

"Slow down," Jaime said, raising his voice. "We can work something out."

"Let's go for a ride," Grant said, and stepped over to squat behind his chair, manipulating the handcuffs. A moment later he stepped back, leveling the heater at him again. "Stand up, and move to the front door."

Jaime rose, his hands free of the chair now but still cuffed behind his back. Grant followed him to the door and out of Truman's field of view. The sound of the buttons on the alarm pad beeping was followed by the door being closed, and then the faint sound of the deadbolt sliding into place.

FOURTEEN

Truman swept the shower curtain aside and hopped out of the bathtub, hustling over to look outside. Grant had backed the Eldorado into the driveway, right up to the door, and as Truman got to the front window, Grant slammed the trunk, and paused to shove the heater into the back of his belt again, then walked casually around to the driver's door, head swiveling as he scanned the dark street. Truman only caught a glimpse of denim and black leather as the lid went down, but it was enough to know that Grant had thrown Jaime in the trunk.

Call the cops, Truman thought. He wasn't in danger himself anymore. He had to call the cops. Still standing at the window, watching Grant pull into the street, he dialed 911. A recording picked up and told him to hold. "Your approximate wait time is three minutes."

Grant would be long gone by then. There were always cops on Sunset, Truman knew, and he could be down there in far less than three minutes. Huffing in frustration, he ended the call and went to the alarm panel, hurriedly turning it off, and then set it again, stepping outside and locking the deadbolt behind him. As he reached the sidewalk, he saw the distinctive taillights of Grant's car at the end of the street, waiting to turn left onto Sunset.

Truman jogged down to the boulevard, watching as Grant made the turn. The bank parking lot where the cops hung out was just a couple of blocks farther, and Truman went through what he was going to tell them. It was so complicated to explain—and he wasn't about to incriminate himself.

On the weekends, before their evening's work on the Strip policing all the drunks at the straight bars and nightclubs, the cops used the parking lot to barbecue and network and strategize. Twilight was almost over—hopefully they were there already.

Sure enough, when he jogged up, there were prowl cars from three different agencies parked on the street, and a handful of uniforms standing around inside the fenced parking lot, smoke wafting skyward from a portable barbecue. Truman trotted up to a cop who was wearing a city uniform, standing at the gate. He was a thickset guy with a dirty-blond crewcut.

"I'm not on duty," the guy said as Truman approached.

"This is important," Truman said, out of breath.

The guy folded his arms. "So call 911."

"I did—they put me on hold. Listen, I just saw a guy handcuff another guy and lock him in the trunk of his car."

The guy sighed, and closed his eyes for a moment. "Did you get a plate number?"

"No," Truman said, but then he remembered. "Wait, yeah, I have a picture." Pulling out his phone, he found the photo he'd taken of Grant's rear license plate.

Another cop, a woman with a dark complexion, her hair pulled tightly back, was standing nearby and listening. When Truman showed the photo to the blond, she stepped closer.

"Why do you have a photo of his plate?" she asked.

"So that you can go after him," Truman said intently. "He's got a gun. I think he wants to kill the guy in the trunk."

The blond squinted at the image on Truman's screen. "That looks like the back end of a Caddy."

"A bright-red Eldorado convertible," Truman

said. "It's a 1973."

"Are you making a film or something?" the guy asked, his eyes narrowing. "I can cite you for wasting police time."

"I'm not lying," Truman said, raising his voice. "If you catch this guy, won't you get a big promotion or a medal or something? I saw him stuff a guy in the trunk of this car."

"Settle down," the woman said.

Truman gestured to the mike clipped on her shoulder. "If you're on dinner break, use your radio brooch and tell someone else to go after him."

The woman exchanged a glance with the blond. "I can check it out," she said finally, and to Truman, "Where did you last see the vehicle?"

"Heading east on Sunset, toward the freeway," Truman said. "Just a minute or two ago. He was near the right-of-way."

She frowned. "The what, now?"

"Where the alleys cross the boulevard at a diagonal." Truman mimed the street layout with his hands. "It's an old railroad right-of-way. There used to be tracks."

"I don't know where that is."

"It's by the Mexican restaurant where all the cops hang out."

"That place, I know," she said, holding his gaze. "Are you sure he was armed?"

"He had a handgun, black and silver, stuffed

in the back of his pants."

She spoke into her shoulder radio and stepped away, gesturing to another guy in uniform. The two of them climbed into a prowl car and pulled out onto Sunset.

"Shouldn't she put the siren on, and the flashing lights?" Truman said to the blond cop, watching them go.

He was practically panting, he realized, and hopped up on adrenaline. At least they'd finally believed him. Maybe he could catch his breath now. He leaned forward and put his hands on his knees, breathing through his nose.

"Can I see your ID?" the cop said.

Truman sighed and straightened up, pulling out his license and handing it over.

"You're Truman?" the cop said, clicking on a little flashlight and studying the card.

"Correct," he said flatly. It was such a stupid question. His name and his photo were right there on the damn card. The cop clicked off the light and then tucked the license away somewhere, and pulled out a notepad.

"Where did you see this happen?"

"In his driveway. Right up the street." Truman gestured vaguely and recited the address.

"What were you doing there?"

"I was, uh, going to visit him." Truman could feel his face heating up.

The cop picked up on his hesitation, his eyes narrowing. "Going to visit the driver, or the guy in the trunk?" he demanded.

"The driver. It's his house."

A cell phone rang, and the cop pulled it out of his pants to look at the screen. "Don't go anywhere," he said to Truman, then stepped through the gate, toward the barbecue with the throng of other uniforms, standing around chatting, holding paper plates and plastic forks.

"How can I?" Truman called after him. "You still have my ID."

But the cop was already focused on his phone, and spent a while in conversation. Truman couldn't overhear what he was saying, but watched him through the fence. It seemed casual, like he was talking to a friend. Finally he cackled and slid the phone into his pants, stepping back to talk to Truman.

"You were right," he said. "They found a guy in the trunk of the Caddy. He was pretty shaken up."

"But he was alive," Truman said, and took a deep breath. "That's good news."

"The driver was a little more trouble. He pointed a weapon at the officers."

"Oh, god," Truman said. "Did you shoot him?"

"They managed to Taser him," the guy said, his eyes narrowing. "Nobody got shot. So how do you know the driver?"

"I met him in a bar. Can I go talk to him?"

The cop guffawed. "Not anytime soon. Right now they're going to book him, and based on what he did, he won't make bail."

"Because he pointed a gun at you?"

"That and the kidnapping. That's a serious offense. He'll be going away for a long time."

"What about—" Truman caught himself before he said *Jaime*—"What about the guy in the trunk?"

"They took him to an ER to get checked out."

"So he'll be out tonight," Truman said.

"No chance. He's in custody too. Before they put him in the ambulance, he set off a facial recognition alert, so they checked his prints. He's wanted in connection to a murder in San Diego." He was watching Truman closely. "Would you know anything about that?"

"That's crazy," Truman said, genuinely surprised. "I never saw the guy before he got stuffed in the trunk. I thought Grant was a real estate agent, not a gun-toting kidnapper."

"Why did you take a photo of his bumper?"

"It's a cool car," Truman said, gesturing vaguely. "Why did you people take a photo of the guy in the trunk?"

The cop pointed to a little black box hanging from the breast pocket of his uniform. "Body cam. It's all automated. Some computer somewhere used facial recognition to match him to a wanted list."

"So you looked up my face too?" Truman said, frowning at the box. It had a little lens in it, he saw now.

"The software would have done that, sure. But I haven't gotten an alert to arrest you yet." He grinned at Truman and winked. "So you were at the driver's house. Why?"

"Sex," Truman said flatly. "We hooked up before, and I was looking to do that again."

The cop nodded, and asked him more questions. Some of them were repetitive, but Truman knew what the guy was doing, because Biff Sturgis used the same techniques—he was trying to catch him contradicting himself or amending the details. *The truth never changes,* Biff said. Truman must have kept the story straight, because the guy finally handed back his ID.

"I can't believe Grant pulled a gun on the cops," Truman said. "That seems crazy."

"You never know about people," he said. "You should always be on your guard. Listen, the detectives will have more questions. What's your phone number?"

As Truman recited it, the cop jotted it in his notebook, then flipped it closed.

"Now that you have my digits," Truman said, "Maybe you could call me after your shift, and we'll go have a coffee."

"I don't think we'll be doing that," he said, eyeing Truman carefully. "Cops and robbers don't mix."

"I'm not a crook," Truman said, raising his voice and scowling at him. "I just helped you catch a crook."

"Thanks for your help, Truman," he said, and grinned as he tucked his notepad away, then walked back through the fence.

Truman headed toward Fairfax, relieved to be done with that. It was cold, he realized, and he pulled his backpack straps tighter. He should have worn a jacket.

At least nobody got iced, and Grant hadn't managed to get himself shot. Truman had misjudged the guy. He seemed so pedestrian, but what he'd been planning to do to Jaime was clear—and he must have been planning it all along. And Jaime—if he'd been popped for a murder rap, Celeste had completely misjudged him too. Pulling out his phone, he dialed her number.

"I never heard back from Jaime," she said when she picked up.

"Forget that. Can you come to Hollywood? Wear something dark."

"Why? What happened? You sound freaked out."

"I'll tell you when you get here."

"Are you OK?" Celeste said carefully.

"I'm just a little rattled."

Truman told her where to meet him, then went to a coffee place and bought a bagel, chewing on it as he walked around the neighborhood, burning off the adrenaline, thinking through what he was going to do next. Celeste was going to be pissed to find out about Jaime, and they needed to talk through the opiates thing, but right now he needed someone he could trust, and Celeste was one of the few people in the world that he trusted unconditionally.

Soon after, Celeste's little blue car pulled up at the curb beside him, and he climbed in the passenger seat. She was wearing jeans and a black turtleneck.

"What's going on?" she demanded, eyeing him as he set his backpack on the floor at his feet.

"Pull around the corner," he said, "and find a place to park."

Once she'd killed the engine, Truman told her the whole story—inadvertently buying heroin at the *paletas* shop, breaking into Grant's house, and dealing with the cops.

As Celeste listened, her eyes grew wider. "They're both goddamn banditos," she said. "Grant could have shot you."

"I was kind of shocked at how quickly things

went south," Truman said. "But he wasn't after me."

"How did they really know each other?"

"They must have worked together. Grant is obviously in the drug trade too. Jaime was wise to avoid him—I'm pretty sure Grant was planning to murdertize him tonight."

"And Jaime's a freaking murderer too," she said.

"The cop said he was wanted in connection with a murder. Maybe he's just a witness to something. Or maybe it's a mistake."

"They don't arrest witnesses," Celeste said flatly. "Don't minimize it, Truman. I knew he was a lowlife."

"It's worse for me," Truman said. "I knew Grant was playing me, but I didn't think he had that in him. Right from the start, he hired me to help him kill somebody."

Celeste was silent for a moment, looking out at the dark street. "We sure can pick 'em."

Truman chuckled. "Still, I can officially declare my first case solved."

"*First* case? You want to go through this again? You could have been shot."

"I'm just getting started, toots. Listen—Grant's house is on the next block. I want to show you something there."

"Don't you think it'll be crawling with cops?"

"Not yet." Truman popped the door and climbed out, slinging on his backpack.

"You can leave your bag, if you want," Celeste said, stepping onto the street.

"Not this time."

Walking up on Grant's house, the light beside the front door was on, and a diffuse warm glow showed through the sheers from the light in the kitchen, but there were no signs of life. Glancing around to make sure they weren't being observed, Truman punched the code into the lock and pushed his way inside, with Celeste close behind. At the alarm panel, he paused to disarm it.

"Why do you have the lock code, and the alarm code?" Celeste asked, closing the door behind her.

"Because Grant underestimated me." Truman went to the front window and drew the drapes, then turned the room lights on.

"This looks like a vacation rental," Celeste said, glancing around.

"I wish you'd been with me when I first came here," Truman said. "It took me forever to figure that out."

"Nice bland place," she said. "But I still think the cops could drop by at any minute. What are we doing here?"

"This," Truman said, and squatted next to the black duffel bag on the carpet. Pulling his shirt-sleeve down over his fingers, he zipped it open without touching the tab.

"Whoa," Celeste said, stepping closer. "That's a lot of freaking money."

"A fuck-ton, Grant said."

Truman hadn't actually seen it before, and took a minute now to look, dropping to his knees. Fat bundles of cash, mostly with C-notes on the outside but with some twenties showing, were folded in half and bound with elastic bands.

"This is what Jaime was taking to San Diego to be exported," Truman said.

"So he's working for a drug cartel. Who else would be exporting that much cash?"

"That seems most likely. It's all used bills too, nothing fresh from the bank."

"At least he wasn't lying about the kind of work he did," she said absently, gazing at the hoard. "He just omitted the part about who he worked for."

"The cops are going to find this eventually," Truman said, looking up at her. "But what if we made it a little lighter?"

"You want to steal from Jaime?" she said, meeting his eye.

"It's not his money. He's just the courier— and it sounds like he's going away for a while. They both are. Why let the cops have it all?"

"Think about what you're saying. You want to steal from a drug cartel. In Mexico they kill people just for looking at them funny."

"Whoever owns this will think the cops seized it," Truman said. "We'll just tax some of it. Grant still owes me, and there's no way he'll be paying me from jail."

"But they'll know," Celeste insisted. "The dollar value will come up in the news, or at the trial. They'll know it's short."

"I thought about that too. Whoever this belongs to doesn't know anything about me. Grant won't suspect me because he doesn't know I was here. He and Jaime are both going to have lots of other things to worry about. Anyone who knows how much is in this bag will just assume the cops took their bite."

"*La mordita,* my father calls it." Celeste sighed and eyed the cash. "How much does Grant owe you?"

"Three-quarters of what's in this bag."

"Bullshit," she said firmly, but then said, "Let's do it. Are we going to count it first?"

"We'll worry about that later," Truman said, and pulled off his backpack, zipping it open. "Let me do the grabbing—my DNA is already all over this house, but yours isn't."

Celeste watched as he rapidly plucked the bundles and dropped them into his bag. Truman's estimate was about right; three-quarters of the duffel bag's contents fit in his backpack. Struggling to zip it closed, he slung it on as he got to his feet.

"Cash is heavy," he said.

"The duffel looks pretty empty now," Celeste said, stepping closer to peer into it.

"It's fine. Let's go."

"You should wipe off the alarm buttons, and the front door lock," she said. "They might look for prints."

"Good idea," Truman said, and then remembered something else. *Never leave behind evidence of your own work.* Stepping into the guest bathroom, he pushed aside the cactus shower curtain and looked in the bottom of the tub. The flawless white surface was marred with his footprints. Hustling into Grant's bedroom, he scooped up a discarded sweatshirt from the floor and went back to the tub, wetting the shirt at the faucet and scrubbing at the dusty marks. Eventually satisfied that it was clean enough, he threw the shirt on the bedroom floor again and then wiped down the alarm panel with his shirtsleeve, as Celeste had suggested. He punched in the code through his cuff so as not to leave any fresh prints, then did the same with the lock on the front door.

Walking back to her car, Celeste looked behind them, turning to rapidly scan the street, even though no one was around. "I get why you didn't want to ride the metro home, hauling a backpack overstuffed with money," she said quietly.

"I also said I'd cut you in when I got paid.

You did part of the work—you should share the payout."

"Or maybe you wanted an accomplice," she said, looping an arm through Truman's.

"A bagman," he said.

"Bagwoman."

"Maybe you're right—I wanted someone to share responsibility for a bad decision."

"'Bad' is a value judgment," Celeste said, stepping into the street and unlocking her car. "No looking back. It's a done deal now."

———◆———

Back at Truman's loft, once he'd locked the deadbolt, standing inside the door, he zipped open the backpack.

"I've never seen so much cash in one place," Celeste said.

"Let's count it."

"On the sofas?"

"It's too easy to lose bills between the cushions."

"I think you can afford it," she said, and frowned, but followed him to the center of the room, sitting cross-legged on the cold concrete.

Truman dumped the contents on the floor, dozens of bundles, and Celeste pushed up the sleeves of her sweater. They started counting, separating the bills by denomination and stacking them in neat piles. It took a while, but eventually they had a total: just over $756,000.

"I guess I don't have to worry about hustling for tour gigs for a while," Truman said, gazing at the stacks.

"A while? You mean, like, ten years."

Truman eyed her. "Ten years each."

She laughed. "I'm glad you roped me into this case. Have you got anything to drink?"

Truman rose and washed his hands in the kitchen sink. All those bills had been in circulation, and undoubtedly carried the germs of thousands of people. In the cupboard he used as a pantry, he found the half-empty bottle of tequila he kept there, and poured a hefty shot of it into each of two tumblers. Next he pulled a lime-flavored Italian soda out of the fridge and split the bottle between the glasses.

"Cowboy margaritas," Truman said, handing her one as he dropped onto the floor beside her.

"Cheers." Celeste clinked her glass on Truman's before she drank, and they both sat there looking at the cash.

"You can't put it in a bank," she said finally. "You have to hide it somewhere."

"Isn't it ten grand that triggers an alert to the tax man?"

"Keep your deposits under two grand. That's the suspicious-activity threshold. And no more than one large deposit a week."

"How do you know that?" Truman demanded.

"My cousin works in a bank," Celeste said, and shrugged. "We talk."

"So where do we stash it?"

"Here." She waved her arm around the loft. "It's the perfect place. You have a heavy door, and the windows are high up. Junkies have never broken in on you before, have they? They'll stick to softer targets."

"I just hope no one ever comes looking for it."

"It seems unlikely that'll happen."

"You're probably right. Do you want to do that money-shower thing you talked about before?"

"I know you'd make me help you clean it up," Celeste said, "so no."

Truman nodded, admiring the stacks. "Not a bad haul for a week's work."